TAVISH SEEKS A WEALTHY BRIDE

ANNA MARKLAND

Dedicated to whisky lovers everywhere.

"What whisky will not cure, there is no cure for."
Old Irish Proverb

ALSO BY ANNA MARKLAND

Anna is a USA Today bestseller who has authored more than sixty award-winning and much-loved Medieval, Viking, Highlander, Elizabethan and Regency historical romances. No matter the historical or geographic setting, many of her series recount the adventures of successive generations of one family, with emphasis on the importance of ancestry and honor. A detailed list with links can be found at https://www.annamarkland.com/

She is an an independent author, so getting the word out about her book is vital to its success. If you enjoy this story, please consider writing a review. Reviews help other readers find books.

Tavish Seeks A Wealthy Bride

Highland Whisky Kings, Book One

© Anna Markland 2024

All rights reserved.

This book is licensed for your personal enjoyment only. It may not be resold or given away to other people. If you would like to share this book with another person, please purchase an additional copy for each recipient. Thank you for respecting the hard work of this author. This book or parts thereof may not be reproduced in any form, stored in any retrieval system, or transmitted in any form by any means—electronic, mechanical, photocopy, recording, or otherwise—without prior written permission of the publisher, except as provided by United States of America copyright law.

This is a work of fiction. Names, characters, places, and incidents either are the products of the author's imagination or are used fictitiously. Any resemblance to actual persons, living or dead, businesses, companies, events, or locales is entirely coincidental.

Cover by Dar Albert

AMBITIOUS PLANS
GLENGEÁRR, SCOTTISH HIGHLANDS, 1811

"Ye'll need coin to finance all yer grand ideas," Uncle Gregor cautioned his nephews.

"Aye, we ken," Tavish King replied. "But Payton, Niven and I have put everything we have into making our whisky the finest money can buy."

"And 'tis the best in the glen as a result," Gregor retorted, rocking back and forth in his favorite chair.

"But there's a bigger market out there than just this remote place," Payton said. "Now, we need investors."

Gregor shook his head. "Yer great, great granddaddy built this distillery hisself. Stone upon stone."

"I seem to recall he had help from his wife," Niven reminded his uncle.

"Aye," Gregor agreed. "And other family. However, ye're missin' the point. His ambition was to distill the finest whisky in this part o' Scotland."

"That was then," Tavish replied. "This is a different century. *Uachdaran* is still the finest single malt to be found hereabouts."

"Clever, that," Gregor said with a chuckle. "Trust a *mon* named King to come up with such a name."

Feeling more exasperated by the minute, Tavish raked his fingers through auburn locks. The distillery wasn't the only thing he'd inherited from his ancestors. "In this valley, we speak the Gaelic, so we know *Uachdaran* means *Sovereign*. There's a big world of people out there who have no idea what it means."

"'Tis the reason we intend to rebrand it as *Sovereign*," Payton declared.

Gregor heaved a sigh. "Rebranding, is it? As well as retrieving our barrels from Spain, harvesting enough peat to keep the kiln fires burnin', acquirin' an agent to market yer whisky in England, transportin' the stuff south o' the border...nay, lads, canna be done without a lot o' coin. And what do Sassenachs ken aboot whisky? They willna like it."

Tavish clenched his jaw, irritated his uncle was probably right. They didn't have the money to implement all their plans for taking *Uachdaran* to a wider market and there was no guarantee the English would buy single malt whisky.

"And another consideration," Gregor said. "Up to now, like most distilleries in the Highlands, ye've operated without a license. Yer landlord has turned a blind eye because he realizes tenants who are in prison canna pay rents."

Tavish clenched his jaw. The two shillings tax on every pint paid mainly by licensed Lowland distilleries had been a sore point for the King family since its imposition in 1644. Not surprisingly, given his cantankerous disposition, the late Walter King had been determined not to pay it. A Highlander paying tax on his whisky! Never! But Tavish reluctantly realized there might come a day when they had no choice. Their reputation was growing and the Earl of Craigdarroch would sooner or later be obliged by the Crown to prosecute them as unlicensed distillers.

"I can only think o' one solution. Ye must all marry into wealthy families," Gregor announced.

Utter silence greeted this pronouncement. Tavish wasn't surprised. He and his two brothers were considered the only eligible bachelors in Glengeárr, which meant that ambitious mothers from miles around with daughters of marriageable age had tried to ensnare the King boys.

As the eldest and majority owner of the distillery, Tavish was the prime target. So far, with his brothers' help, he'd managed to avoid the traps set for him.

"I hate to say it," Niven finally murmured, "but Uncle's right. Tavish needs a wealthy wife."

"Nay, all o' ye must marry. Ye need a passel o' sons to run this business and keep the traditions alive after ye're gone."

"And where do ye suggest we find wealthy women in Glengeárr?" Payton asked.

Gregor heaved himself up from the rocking chair and brandished his rams-head staff. "Fer lads wi' such grand ambitions, ye're nay verra bright."

The King brothers had been brought up to respect their elders, but Tavish chafed at the insult. "And what do ye mean by that?" he demanded.

"'Tis a sad truth that Glengeárr isna where ye'll find the wealth ye need. I'd venture to say ye willna find it in the whole o' Scotland."

"So, where is this wonderful Utopia full o' rich lasses?" Tavish asked sarcastically.

"London," Gregor replied with a disturbing twinkle in his eyes.

"Surely, Uncle, ye dinna expect us to wed Sassenachs?" Tavish spluttered.

"At five and twenty," Gregor replied. "Ye're the eldest. 'Tis time to think o' startin' a family in any case."

"But we canna wed Englishwomen," Payton retorted angrily.

"'Twould simply be the dowries ye'd be after," Gregor explained patiently. "Ye dinna have to like yer wives, or e'en bring 'em back to Scotland."

The prospect of a hefty dowry appealed to Tavish, but a loveless marriage sounded too much like his parents' arrangement. He'd avoided matrimony because he hadn't found a lass he liked enough to consider as a life partner. He'd never confess his longing for a loving relationship to his devil-may-care brothers who relished the game of outwitting prospective mothers-in-law. He decided to poke holes in his uncle's plan. "And how do ye propose we go about insinuating ourselves into London society?"

"It pains me to suggest it," Gregor replied. "And 'tis only as a last resort, ye ken."

Tavish had an inkling now about the twinkle in his uncle's eyes. "Ye mean to contact yer sister."

Niven snorted. "The one ye swore never to speak to agin after she ran away wi' a Sassenach."

"Aye, weel, needs must," Gregor muttered. "Maureen's wed to some lordling or other. She could introduce ye to the right folk."

"And what makes ye think she'll agree?" Tavish asked.

"She said so in her response to my letter."

∼

FOR THIRTY YEARS, Gregor had regretted cutting off all contact with his sister, but what was a man to do when his sibling ran off and married an Englishman? He'd warned Maureen she'd be sorry but, in his heart, he hoped she'd had a happy life with Freddie Hawkins. The man was rich, so she'd probably been comfortable.

He prayed she'd fared better than their other sister who'd ignored everyone's advice and insisted on marrying Walter King, a local man nobody liked. Moira had led an unhappy life and turned into a shrew. The only good thing to come out of that marriage was the birth of three strapping sons.

It was perhaps better to let sleeping dogs lie as far as his errant sister was concerned, but he had to do something to help his nephews. He'd never had any bairns of his own. Walter King's death had been a blessing. Gregor's brother-in-law was a poor excuse of a man who beat his sons, whereas Gregor was happy to watch over and see them grow and thrive.

What Tavish and his brothers had achieved by

expanding and improving the methods of an ancient distillery was nothing short of miraculous. Gregor intended to do every thing in his power to help them fulfill their dreams—even if it meant groveling to his estranged sister. At least she'd replied to his missive.

LONDON

RAMSAY HOUSE, MAYFAIR, LONDON

Dowager Duchess Maureen Hawkins fanned herself with the latest missive from the brother who'd disowned her thirty years ago. "Typical Scot," she muttered to her son and daughter. "Gregor deigns to correspond with me now he needs something."

"The Kings are still coming, then?" Kenneth, Duke of Ramsay, asked.

"Aye," she replied.

Her irritating lapse into the brogue she'd worked hard to banish caused Kenneth to raise a brow.

"My nephews arrive in a fortnight," she added, hoping to distract him.

"Do you remember them?" her daughter asked.

"Born after I left Scotland with your father," she replied with a shake of her head. "But their parents were an odd pair. Couldn't stand each other. My sister never did have much common sense."

"We're not expecting much, then," Kenneth said.

"No. Probably a bunch of uncouth Highlanders. They're coming to investigate a wider market for their whisky."

"They operate a distillery?" Daisy asked.

"A primitive stone building, if I recall correctly. I'm surprised it hasn't fallen down."

Kenneth's eyes widened. "Is the whisky good?"

"I never tasted it. Young women weren't allowed to imbibe in those days."

Kenneth rubbed his hands together. "Let's hope they bring a bottle or two. I'm rather partial to a good single malt now and again."

"I thought you were a brandy man."

"I am, but Prinny has a taste for all things Scottish. It's the *ton's* latest fad. Besides which, Napoleon's thirst for power has made French brandy almost impossible to obtain. Whatever is smuggled in costs a pretty penny."

"That's all well and good, but Gregor expects me to introduce these boys to our friends and acquaintances. I've been thinking that hosting a ball here at the main house is the simplest way. Three weeks from today, let's say. I'll get my secretary working on invitations and so on. We must pray my nephews' attire consists of more than kilts and Argyll socks."

"I've never seen a man in a kilt," Daisy murmured.

∽

KENNETH BREATHED MORE EASILY after leaving the Dower House. Throughout the interview, his mother hadn't once dredged up her favorite topic. The impending visit of these King cousins from the Highlands seemed to have taken her mind off the knotty problem of his unmarried status.

He accepted he had an obligation to marry and provide heirs for the Dukedom of Ramsay. However, there was no rush. He enjoyed his bachelor life. It would be entertaining to squire his Scottish cousins about town.

The latest candidate his mother had found for him might prove to be an acceptable wife. If only Priscilla Graham wouldn't insist on being known by the nickname bestowed by her Scottish grandfather. A duchess named Piper! It was out of the question.

She'd surely be reasonable about it, though he hadn't yet been able to dissuade her. Perhaps if he actually offered marriage.

He'd give more thought to that after the Kings went back to Scotland. If their product turned out to be halfway decent, he might introduce them to his man of business.

In the meantime, they had two weeks to organize a schedule of social events for the visitors. Hosting a ball was a good idea, except that his mother would no doubt invite Priscilla and expect him to dance attendance on her all evening. The notion of introducing his cousins as the Highland Whisky Kings lightened his mood a little. Daisy seemed pleased with the prospect of meeting them.

"Aren't you going to open it?"

Seated on the sofa in the parlor of her parents' London townhouse, Piper Graham stared at the elegantly engraved envelope in her hands. She hadn't heard from Kenneth Hawkins in over a week. How to explain to her matchmaking mother that she'd hoped the duke had decided to drop his suit. The missive was from the Dowager Duchess but the envelope clearly contained an invitation.

"It came with ours," Lady Graham announced, eyes bright with expectation. "It's to Ramsay House."

Piper wanted to believe her parents would never push her into an unwanted marriage, but it was clear they thought Kenneth Hawkins was heaven sent. If their daughter married him, she would become a duchess. Kenneth was kind, generous, titled and ruggedly handsome—and Piper hoped they'd always be friends. However, she dreamed of meeting a passionate lover, a man who would cherish her. Kenneth was rather staid and stuffy, and her mother would never understand a desire for a marriage based on mutual love. Perhaps such a thing wasn't to be found and she was being overly naive.

Dithering served no purpose, so she tore open the envelope. "It *is* an invitation to Ramsay House," she confirmed.

"Perhaps an occasion for an announcement," her smiling mother suggested.

Piper was relieved to naysay that possibility. "Apparently, it's to welcome some cousins of the Hawkins family, visiting from Scotland."

Lady Graham's smile fled. "Oh, dear," she murmured. "Scotland. I didn't read that detail."

Piper thought it high time her very English mother got over her dislike of her Scottish father-in-law. In Piper's estimation, Grandad Jock was a fine fellow but, for some unknown reason, he and Margaret Graham had never seen eye to eye.

Since her invitation had come separately and both were from the Dowager Duchess, Piper saw no harm in accepting, although it was Maureen Hawkins who'd finagled to introduce her and Kenneth to each other.

Still, meeting cousins from Scotland sounded more interesting than most of the balls her mother insisted she attend.

∼

OLIVER GRAHAM still loved his wife to distraction, though he sometimes doubted his own sanity. From the beginning, he'd been reluctant to admit that Margaret didn't love him, but he'd ignored his father's warnings about loveless marriages and married her anyway.

She soon tired of his native Galloway where they'd met when she visited a distant cousin. She deemed all Scots provincial and uneducated, despite the fact he'd attended Eton and graduated *magna cum laude* from Oxford.

He eventually gave in to her constant whining about returning to London where she'd been born. Prudent investments of family money had provided them with an opulent lifestyle. They lacked for nothing, but Margaret never seemed satisfied.

The best thing to come of their marriage was Priscilla. His daughter was intelligent and beautiful, but she was a free spirit. She preferred to be called Piper, a nickname Oliver's father had bestowed when last he and his daughter visited Galloway. He agreed that Priscilla wasn't a name that suited her. Margaret hated the nickname, probably because Jock Graham had come up with it. She was determined to marry their daughter off to a titled gentleman. Sooner or later, Margaret's rigid societal expectations and Piper's wish to live life by her own rules would collide. Then Oliver would have to make an impossible decision and side with either his wife or his daughter.

THE WHITE HORSE

The Kings arrived in Edinburgh soaking wet. It had rained throughout the taxing journey from Glengeárr. The tarpaulin thrown over the wagon normally used for hauling barrels and crates had provided scant shelter when they'd camped overnight, and none at all during the long days. Tavish began to doubt the wisdom of traveling all the way to London, especially since Uncle Gregor had decided to accompany them.

"Just to keep an eye, ye ken," he'd said.

They could hardly object when he offered to pay the £4 mail coach fare for each of them. They had no idea where he might have laid his hands on such a sum. It was even more surprising that he was willing to part with it!

However, the overnight Royal Mail would get them to the capital city in a fraction of the time any other means of transport could promise, so they weren't about to argue.

On the way to Edinburgh, they'd trudged through mud and lent shoulders to dislodge wagon wheels bogged down in deep ruts. Auld Jamie, who'd worked as the driver for the King family for decades, frequently voiced the gruff opinion they were on a fools' errand. "Naught good e'er came from London."

As they might have expected, the sun appeared the moment they arrived at the *White Horse Inn* and there wasn't a cloud in the sky. Jamie chuckled loudly as he drove away to the stables, leaving them outside the inn, steam rising from their hair. "'Twould serve him right if he encounters a blizzard on the way home," Tavish muttered under his breath, resentful of gaping passers-by.

"Let's get inside," Payton suggested, hefting the wet luggage. Niven took charge of the crate of whisky they planned to smuggle aboard.

When they entered the inn's foyer, heads turned. Some folk sniggered.

"I assume they've ne'er seen wet travelers afore," Niven said.

"I think it has more to do with our kilts," Payton countered. "And the fact no one else looks like a drowned rat."

"Aye," Gregor sighed. "'Tis the rare *mon* who wears a kilt in Edinburgh. More's the pity."

Tavish wasn't sure how his uncle knew this since he'd never traveled outside Glengeárr in his life. However, while he was pondering, Gregor marched up to the innkeeper and gruffly announced their needs—a room, a hot meal and a bath.

To the King brothers' surprise, this direct approach worked.

"And how long will ye be staying?" the landlord asked.

"Till the mail coach leaves fer London," Gregor replied.

"Two days then."

"Aye."

"I can ensure ye have seats inside, if ye wish."

"Good o' ye," Gregor replied, pulling a wad of bank notes from his leather sporran.

The Kings exchanged a wide-eyed glance of astonishment.

The innkeeper eyed the wad. "For four o' ye, that's £20."

Gregor scowled. "Nay, £16."

"Plus a small fee fer arranging yer comfort. And I can make sure the guard turns a blind eye to yon crate."

"I reckon £4 is nay a small fee. I'll gi' ye £18 and that should cover the cost o' the room as weel as safe passage for the crate."

He peeled off the notes, pressed them to the gaping innkeeper's chest, relieved him of the key in his hand and demanded to be shown to the room.

"Maybe 'tis a good thing Uncle came along, after all," Niven said with a grin as they followed a scruffy urchin tasked with showing them the way.

"I dinna have great expectations," Tavish muttered as they negotiated the alarmingly creaky, narrow wooden staircase to the third floor.

He was pleasantly surprised when the room turned

out to be spacious and clean, though peeling plaster hinted at pervasive damp.

The lad knelt to strike a spark to the kindling under the coal fire already laid in the hearth.

"And to think," Gregor declared as they removed sodden plaids. "Mary, Queen o' Scots stayed in this very inn. 'Twas named fer her favorite nag."

"I doot this room's been plastered since," Payton quipped.

Gregor glared. "Ye ha'e no sense o' history."

"Just sayin' could do wi' a coat o' whitewash," Payton retorted.

Tavish was more concerned about the presence of only two beds, so he took advantage of the distraction. "Niven and I will tek this one," he said as he sat on the thin mattress and toed off a boot.

Payton sulked.

Tavish shrugged. It was his right as the eldest to decide who slept where. Gregor snored loudly on the frequent occasions he fell asleep sitting upright in his rocking chair. He doubted anybody but their uncle would get much sleep this night.

"I'll tell the scullery lads to bring up a bath," the lad said, still with an eye on the fledgling fire. "But me Da willna let me bring ye victuals. Insists ye come doon to the dining room."

"Reet," Tavish replied, deeming it a waste of effort to argue with the lad who was only doing his father's bidding. "Bath first, if ye please, then we'll find the dining room. Lots o' hot water, mind."

"Sir," came the polite reply. "Cormac's the name."

"Much as I want to be out o' these wet togs," Gregor said after the boy left. "I dinna want to stand aboot in the altogether while we wait for the bath to arrive."

"True, Uncle," Payton said, winking at Tavish. "Might give the lads a shock to see four Highlanders stark naked."

Tavish could have teased his uncle. The King brothers didn't necessarily want to watch Gregor strutting about unclothed, but the man had no sense of humor. "Weel, I'm for being ready when the water arrives," he said, peeling off his socks. Then he stood, unbuckled his kilt and let it fall. The woollen jacket came next, leaving him clad in just his long shirt with the ruffles at the neck.

Payton and Niven agreed and the three brothers were soon almost naked. Gregor dithered, which guaranteed he wouldn't get first dibs on the bath when it arrived.

They heard the racket of the metal tub being carried up the stairs long before it was actually heaved through the door by four scruffy boys who looked about ten years old.

The Kings had never hired bairns under the age of thirteen to work in the distillery, though a few widows had pleaded with them to take on young sons, and even daughters. Distilling fine whisky took experience and finesse. The men they relied on had worked for the family for years, some since their father's time. The handful of adolescents in the Kings' employ were sons anxious to learn their father's skills. Bairns shouldn't be expected to be breadwinners.

"Brought a maiden," Cormac announced, unfolding the wooden frame in front of the fire.

"Thoughtful o' ye," Gregor replied. "Our togs will dry in no time now."

The four lads deposited the galvanized tub and quickly disappeared, hopefully to fetch water.

Cormac eyed the clothing scattered about the floor and began picking up kilts and socks, which he draped over the maiden. Frowning when he evidently didn't find an item he was seeking, he asked, "Ye dinna wear drawers?"

"Nay," Gregor replied, pulling his shirt tails out of his kilt. "Long enough to wrap betwixt the legs and protect the family jewels."

The reappearance of the bucket-toting scullery lads distracted Cormac from his gobsmacked stare and the King brothers from their grinning amusement.

Tavish had his shirt off and was in the tub before the sweating lads left. As the hot water seeped into his bones, he was grateful. As the firstborn son of Moira and Walter King, he'd often borne the brunt of his parents' unhappiness with their lot in life. He loved Payton and Niven and had protected his younger siblings from their father's fists. However, it was smugly satisfying that, by the time everyone else got to bathe, the water would be tepid at best.

After soaping up and rinsing most of his body, he turned his attention to his male parts. His uncle insisted he didn't even have to like the woman he married, but he hoped that wouldn't be the case. Intimacy with a wife just for the sake of siring bairns held no appeal. If he had to marry, he'd like a feisty lass who loved him. But that was a foolish dream, though his manhood wholeheartedly approved of the notion.

As he might have expected, his scoffing brothers didn't fail to notice his arousal when he got out of the tub.

The teasing grins fled when Gregor took advantage of their distraction and plopped down in the tub with a loud splash that sent water cascading over the sides.

YELLOW ROSES

The morning after the arrival of the invitation to Ramsay House, Piper sensed as soon as she reached the bottom of the stairs that something else had caused the flush reddening her mother's face.

"You simply must see the roses," Lady Graham cooed, linking her arm.

Piper had no doubt they would be yellow tea roses and wished she'd never confided her favorite flower to Kenneth Hawkins.

The lavish bouquet sat squarely in the center of the table in the breakfast nook. Clearly, her mother wanted to make sure she didn't overlook it, nor the small attached envelope. She opened it, read the brief message scrawled on the card and put it down on the table.

"What does it say?"

Piper suspected her mother had already sneaked a peek inside the unsealed envelope, so she may as well reveal the contents. "The Duke of Ramsay informs me he will call later today and hopes I'll accompany him on a ride through Hyde Park."

"Thrilling," her mother gushed. "Don't you think so, Dear?"

Hidden behind *The Times*, Oliver Graham merely grunted.

"I planned to meet Carolyn and Esther at the Circulating Library this afternoon," Piper lied.

"Nonsense," her mother replied as she took her place at the table. "You have a duke interested in pursuing you, yet you want to avoid him and spend time with your frivolous friends. I do not understand you at all."

Piper resented the slur cast upon her dearest chums and didn't know what to make of another grunt from behind *The Times*. Did her father not understand her either, or was he censuring his wife's outburst? Was Papa an ally, or…?

"I like Kenneth Hawkins," she tried. "I simply don't want to marry him."

"Of course not," her mother replied, eyes narrowed. "You refuse to lift this family out of genteel poverty because you harbor romantic notions in that silly head of yours."

Suddenly, *The Times* crumpled to her father's lap. "Steady on, Margaret," he groused. "Genteel poverty's a bit much."

Piper felt the walls closing in. The Grahams were far from poor. They lived in an opulent townhouse in the best neighborhood. They ate fine food, wore tailored clothing, employed an army of competent servants and rode about town in expensive carriages.

Their stables were full of prime horseflesh and no merchant ever declined them credit. It wasn't the fact she was facing the prospect of marriage to a man she didn't love that had upset her father. The insinuation they were in financial difficulty had offended his sensibilities.

∼

As Kenneth had a right to expect, the front door of the Graham townhouse was opened to him before he knocked. "Your Grace," the butler said, bowing politely. "May I take your hat?"

"Higgins," Kenneth acknowledged, doffing his beaver and peeling off his kidskin gloves.

"Your Grace," Lady Graham gushed, appearing just as Kenneth was handing his hat and gloves to the butler.

He was disappointed Priscilla hadn't come to greet him first, but perhaps it was more appropriate for her mother to do so.

"Oh, the roses are magnificent, Your Grace," his hostess exclaimed, taking his arm.

Kenneth flinched at the overly familiar gesture. Surely the woman didn't think he'd sent the bouquet to her? "Your daughter did receive them?" he asked, annoyed he'd had to seek confirmation like some overeager youth.

"She's waiting for you in the parlor," came the reply as she pulled him along. "Tea before you embark on your adventure?"

It would be impolite to refuse the offer of a beverage,

though he'd prefer to be off to Hyde Park. "Of course, delightful," he replied.

"Tea, Higgins," Lady Graham called to the butler as they entered the parlor.

Priscilla rose from the settee and curtseyed prettily. She was a vision of loveliness in a skirt and jacket of purple velvet that matched the color of her intriguing eyes. The frilly collar of a snow-white blouse caressed her long neck. Her glorious chestnut hair was done up in some sort of bun arrangement. Appropriate, he supposed for a ride in the park, though he'd be curious to see it down around her shoulders one day. He didn't quite know what to make of her frown. Was she anxious to be alone with him and resented the delay?

Or had she not liked the roses?

Impossible.

He chose to believe she was looking forward to spending the afternoon with him.

"My dear Miss Graham," he said, taking her hand to help her rise. "No need for formality."

When her mother cleared her throat, he realized belatedly he'd touched her daughter's cold hand without gloves. "Sorry," he muttered, deliberately compounding the offense by lifting it to his lips and bestowing a courtly kiss. He was a duke, after all.

"Your Grace," Priscilla whispered, quickly withdrawing her hand. "Won't you take a seat?"

He'd hoped to sit beside her but she'd indicated an armchair across from the settee. Confident the ladies had taken notice of the quality of his blue superfine frock coat, he made a show of flipping up the tails before he eased himself into the chair. Priscilla had a good view of his custom-tailored buff breeches so he crossed his legs and decided that sitting across from her was for the best.

A maid wheeled in the tea trolley, and the ritual began. He'd never understood what people loved about the wretched libation. Like his Scottish mother, he could only tolerate it with copious amounts of sugar added.

∽

Piper had to admit her visitor knew how to dress to his advantage. The blue coat matched his eyes. His valet must have spent hours polishing his hessians. The buff breeches clung to his long, well-muscled legs. Perhaps she was being foolish. If she married Kenneth Hawkins, she'd become a duchess. If she didn't, the passion she craved might never come along. Then where would she be? An aging spinster still pining for true love.

"Thank you for the roses," she said, realizing she should have said something earlier.

"My pleasure," he replied, grimacing as he sipped his tea.

"Is the Darjeeling not to your liking?" she asked, earning a glare from her spluttering mother.

"More sugar perhaps," he replied.

Piper cringed. He'd already stirred in three heaping teaspoons of the sweetener. Clearly, he had no love for the taste of the tea itself.

"Personally," she began, pleased to discover something she had in common with him. "I have never acquired a taste for tea."

"Nor I," he confessed with a smile that revealed two charming dimples and silenced her mother's gasping. "I suppose we drink it because it's the fashionable thing to do."

"Is coffee more to your liking, Your Grace?" her mother inquired. "I'll summon Higgins."

"No, thank you, Lady Graham," he replied as he set down his cup and saucer on the side table and stood. "Forgive my rudeness, but I prefer to get our ride underway before the riff-raff descends on the park."

Piper accepted his surprisingly warm hand to rise. It was the first male hand she'd ever really touched without gloves—apart from her father and grandfather. Kenneth's grip was strong and gentle at the same time. She started to think a ride with the Duke of Ramsay might turn out to be a pleasant outing after all.

THE MAIL COACH

All things considered, *The White Horse* wasn't a bad place to stay. Cormac kept the fire going and the food was decent. After the second day's evening meal, Tavish and his brothers packed up and hurried outside to watch the mail sacks being loaded into the secure rear compartment of the overnight Royal Mail coach.

The smartly liveried guard then proceeded to assemble his arsenal—a blunderbuss and two pistols. Anxious to be on their way, the Kings had left Gregor to settle with the landlord, but Tavish found the display of weaponry disturbing.

"I swear," Payton declared, apparently unfazed by the possibility of highway robbery. "If Uncle snores like a rip saw all the way to London..."

"'Tis guaranteed he will," Niven replied.

"Here he comes," Tavish warned. "Hopefully, our Aunty Maureen's house is big enough for him to be given his own room."

"All arranged, lads," Gregor announced, thrusting his bag at the startled driver. "Inside as promised."

Huddled around the coach, the small crowd of fellow passengers glared. If the Kings occupied the four seats inside, the rest would have to travel on the roof or beside the driver. It was common knowledge that outside riders sometimes tumbled off the coach or froze to death in the winter. Tavish could put up with his uncle's snoring if it meant traveling inside in relative warmth and comfort.

"If a *mon* in a kilt rides on yon roof," Gregor declared loudly, "there's scant chance o' arriving in London with the family jewels still in good lick."

The hostile glares turned to snarls.

"'Tis a good thing the coach doesna stop en route," Payton said. "One o' our fellow travelers might kill 'im."

Gregor had apparently overheard at least part of the remark. "The coach will need to stop to change 'osses, and to collect the mail."

"I heard they dinna stop for the mail," Niven replied. "They just chuck the sacks o' letters."

"Somebody's been pulling yer leg," Gregor retorted, heaving himself aboard when the driver opened the door.

When he boarded, Tavish was pleasantly surprised by the spotlessly clean, well-upholstered gray interior. There was plenty of leg room, even for three tall Highlanders. They were relieved to see their precious crate tucked into a corner. The innkeeper had kept his part of the bargain.

Ten hours later, he was sorely tempted to throttle his uncle who'd fallen asleep before the coach even left *The*

White Horse and snored loudly ever since. He'd been impossible to rouse even when everyone else had to alight and help push the coach up a particularly steep hill. The full moon illuminated the haggard faces of the outside passengers. The guard's impressive maroon and gold livery had wilted.

Tavish and his yawning brothers took care of nature's call during the brief stops to change horses and drivers but Gregor apparently had a more ample bladder.

They rarely stopped to pick up mail. The guard threw the sacks off the coach and snatched the new deliveries from the postmaster. Tavish doubted his uncle would believe it if they told him once he woke.

Periodically, the guard blew a horn to alert the post house to the imminent arrival of the coach and warn tollgate keepers to open the gate. This seemed to occur every time they had finally dozed off.

"Uncle told me mail coaches are exempt from paying tolls," a sleepy Niven informed them. "A fine results if the coach is forced to stop."

Dawn brought out vendors at some of the exchanges. Tavish bought pasties, chuckling along with his brothers when Gregor stretched awake and grabbed a pasty. "I'm nay really hungry," he claimed. "Didna sleep a wink."

It was almost noon by the time they reached the outskirts of London. Tavish hoped to purchase more pasties, but only boiled eggs and day-old bread were available at subsequent exchanges. Nevertheless, it was better than nothing.

"What's that smell?" Payton asked, wrinkling his nose. "Worse than Edinburgh."

"Too many people living too close together," Tavish replied, already missing the fresh air of the Highlands. "Or mayhap our uncle's plumbing has finally started to work."

Mid-afternoon saw them tumble out of the coach at the Gloucester Coffee House on Piccadilly. Exhausted, Tavish had no idea how to proceed, so he was grateful Gregor was suddenly wide awake. "Dinna fash," his uncle assured them. "Maureen instructed me to get a hackney."

In short order, he'd flagged down a vehicle and directed the driver to Ramsay House. "I dinna ken the street," he told the cabbie who stared at him as if he were daft before informing them he knew where it was.

"I suppose 'twould be the same if a body came to Glengeárr and asked for our distillery," Payton suggested with a shrug.

Tavish nodded his agreement though it occurred to him London was a wee bit bigger than their home town.

∽

GREGOR HAD NEVER TRAVELED outside the highland glen where he'd lived his whole life. He'd felt out of his element in Edinburgh, but London was a different matter entirely. The stench alone was enough to put a man off his food for a week—piss and horse droppings unless he missed his guess. There were piles of refuse in the middle of the street!

Looking around for a hackney, he espied ragged urchins begging on every corner of Piccadilly.

The cacophony of noise was deafening—street vendors, a multitude of speeding carriages going in all different directions, men shouting to no one in particular for no apparent reason. He was heartily relieved when he finally managed to flag down a hackney, though he almost had to clobber the nag with his staff.

He couldn't allow his nephews to sense any uncertainty on his part. They were depending on him and he wasn't going to let his lads down.

The hackney eventually left the crowded city streets behind. The neighborhoods looked more prosperous. Freddie Hawkins came from a wealthy family, but there was no guarantee he'd done well in life. Gregor could only hope his sister's house was reasonably comfortable.

HYDE PARK

"The rain seems to be holding off," Kenneth said as they entered Hyde Park. It rankled that a man proud of his reputation as a brilliant conversationalist had resorted to uttering a trite remark about the weather. He wasn't sure why he felt nervous. His barouche and the magnificent matched grays in the traces drew envious stares. His companion was a beautiful, elegantly dressed woman whose smile indicated she was enjoying the ride. His own outfit was impeccably tailored. He'd acknowledged every greeting along the way with the appropriate amount of attention. The Grahams had sent along a maid as chaperone for their daughter.

Everything was as it should be, yet he was uncomfortable.

"Not a cloud in sight, Your Grace," Priscilla replied, looking up at the sky.

Once they married, he could rain kisses the length of her long neck. That thought ought to have aroused interest in his nether regions but, alas, his member failed to stir. Perhaps the prospect of marriage was simply making him too anxious.

Perplexed, he sought to banish the puzzled frown from her lovely face. "I think it's time we were less formal with each other. Please feel free to address me as Ramsay."

He wasn't sure why that generous offer seemed to deepen her dismay, but he soldiered on. "And, with your permission, I'll call you Priscilla."

"As I told you, I prefer Piper, Your Grace," she replied curtly, turning away from him.

This clearly wasn't the time to discuss the unsuitable nickname she seemed determined to cling to. In an effort to draw her attention away from the passing crowds, he thought to mention his cousins. "The Kings are on their way," he announced.

She swiveled to face him, but the frown remained. "Kings?" she asked.

Heat flooded his face. Could he have made a more confusing statement?

"Er…my cousins. Their family name is King. From Scotland."

"Oh," she replied.

"The ball is in their honor."

"Yes, so I'll get to meet them, I suppose," she said without much enthusiasm.

The knot in his gut loosened. At least she'd agreed to attend the ball.

Piper chewed her bottom lip, struggling to hold her tongue. If she and Kenneth Hawkins married, would she be expected to address him as *Ramsay* when they were engaged in sexual congress? The notion was almost laughable if it weren't so pathetic.

And exactly what was wrong with wanting to be called *Piper*? He clearly found the nickname offensive. Well, she found the prospect of addressing him by his ducal title equally offensive. It wasn't as if the Hawkins family had been dukes forever. The unexpected deaths of several cousins had resulted in Kenneth's father inheriting the dukedom. However, none of that history mattered to Piper's mother. A duke was a duke.

She regretted that her reaction had obviously upset Kenneth. He was a genuinely nice man who'd put a lot of effort into impressing her with this outing. The carriage ride and the roses indicated he was serious about pursuing her. Judging by the gasps of dismay and clucking sounds emanating from the back seat, her maid also thought she'd been rude.

But how could she explain to a man she barely knew that she thirsted to fall head over heels in love? He'd be insulted if she told him she saw him only as a friend.

He'd likely consider her a foolish nitwit.

Perhaps he'd be right.

~

"I'm pleased you plan to attend the ball," Kenneth told Priscilla. "Mother and I thought it the most expedient way to introduce my cousins to the *ton*."

"Why have they decided to make the long journey?" she asked.

"They own a distillery in Scotland and apparently need investors to fund improvements."

"A distillery?" she asked, amethyst eyes wide as saucers.

Kenneth was glad to see she'd apparently recovered from her pout. But what was so exciting about a distillery? "Whisky," he explained.

"My grandfather loves whisky," she exclaimed, smiling broadly. "Of course, he's a Scot."

His spirits lifted. "You know my mother is Scottish too."

"I thought I detected a wee trace of a brogue," she said with a chuckle.

The breath hitched in Kenneth's throat. It was the unexpected topic of Scotch whisky that had led to the easiest conversation he'd had with Priscilla Graham.

Perhaps his cousins' visit might pave the way for his suit to succeed.

∽

OLIVER WAS WORKING in his study when Margaret burst in. Red eyes and a kerchief clutched in one hand told him she'd been crying. It wasn't unusual behavior but Oliver leaped to his feet to embrace her, cursing that he indulged her histrionics. "What's amiss?" he asked.

"Oh, I'm just so happy Priscilla is out with her gentleman."

He sensed that Piper had no love for *her gentleman,*

but his wife was already upset so he didn't want to start an argument he couldn't win. There had to be more to this display of tears. She'd eventually tell him.

"His Grace doesn't like tea," she wailed, dabbing her eyes with the kerchief.

Oliver was at a loss. "And you're upset about this because..."

"Don't you see? We must order more coffee. We simply don't have enough to serve him his preferred beverage every time he calls on Priscilla."

Oliver doubted coffee was Ramsay's *preferred beverage*, but he gave in, as he always did. "Of course," he said. "I'll see to it."

WELCOME TO RAMSAY HOUSE

No one riding in the hackney said a word, but Tavish felt the tension mount when the vehicle turned off an incredibly wide, tree-lined avenue in a neighborhood far removed from the crowded center of the city. Leaving behind mansions that looked big enough to house the entire population of Glengeárr, they continued along a winding driveway.

"Clearly doesna ken where he is," Gregor finally muttered, readying his staff to rap on the roof.

Tavish stayed his hand. "Wait," was all he could say as the hackney came to a halt outside a magnificent house.

"This canna be right," Gregor exclaimed, as they gazed up at what could only be described as a five story palace.

"So many chimneys," Niven murmured. "Do ye suppose every one o' them serves a fireplace?"

"This is the wrong place," Gregor insisted. "I ken Maureen married a lordling, but..."

"Welcome," a liveried footman exclaimed as he opened the door of the hackney. "You gentlemen have had a long journey from Scotland."

"Aye," Gregor replied, pulling out his wad of banknotes after he was assisted from the cab.

Another man appeared—older and more formally dressed. "Harrison at your service. I'm His Grace's butler. James Footman will take care of your driver."

After being helped to navigate the steps of the hackney, the brothers gaped at the army of servants who'd appeared to carry their bags. "His Grace?" Tavish muttered.

"Mrs. Harrison is our housekeeper," the butler explained, gesturing to an older, pear-shaped woman who waddled out of the house. "She'll show you to your chambers. No relation, I hasten to add."

"A moment," Gregor said. "My sister? Is she…"

"The Dowager Duchess has invited you to the Dower House for dinner, but she thought you'd like to freshen up and change beforehand. You'll be comfortable here at the main house. More guest chambers and other modern facilities, you understand."

Rendered speechless by the opulence of the house's enormous foyer, the Kings and their uncle pulled up their drooping socks and trudged after the housekeeper like a bunch of woolly sheep following the dominant ewe. Keeping an eye on the bewigged servants carrying their baggage, Tavish looked back to the entryway, relieved they hadn't left a trail of mucky footprints across the polished tiles.

On the second floor, Mrs. Harrison thrust open the

door to a chamber. "For the Dowager's brother," she announced.

The Kings exchanged a wary smile as they followed their uncle into a huge bedroom with a gigantic four-poster on a raised dais in the center of the chamber. The green velvet drapery must have cost a fortune.

Gregor hesitated. "I dinna understand. My sister doesna live here?"

"Duchess Maureen moved into the Dower House after her late husband's death," Mrs. Harrison explained. "Her son is now the Duke of Ramsay."

"But Freddie Hawkins wasna a duke when they eloped," Gregor exclaimed. "And I didna ken her husband had died. I ha'e another nephew?"

Mrs. Harrison's face soured as if she'd bitten into a lemon. Evidently, she was uncomfortable with these personal details. "And a niece. However, I'm sure the Dowager will address your concerns. If you'll follow me," she commanded the brothers. "I'll show you gentlemen to your chambers."

Astonished as he was by the unexpected grandeur of the house, Tavish chuckled inwardly. They'd never imagined their London relatives were so wealthy and doubtless well connected. Luxurious living would take some getting used to, but he resolved to make the most of it.

~

"Will I do, Sims?" Kenneth asked.

"Satisfactory, Your Grace," his valet intoned. "I'm

sure your cousins will be impressed with your formal dinner attire."

Kenneth was certain his valet did not realize he'd given voice to an uncertainty lurking in his master's heart. He'd yet to meet his visiting relatives who'd declined the offer of a valet's services. It seemed his Uncle Gregor had pointed out in no uncertain terms he was perfectly capable of helping his lads dress.

Apparently, the uncle who'd shunned Kenneth's mother thirty years ago was still the ornery character he'd been then.

The "lads"—Kenneth's cousins—were the unknown quantity. Had he dressed too formally? Would they be embarrassed and think him a pompous English nobleman? And why should their opinion matter? They hailed from a remote Scottish glen in the Highlands and were perhaps uneducated. They distilled whisky—probably illegally. Was it the uncle who'd come up with the foolish notion they could expand their market south of the border? Englishmen favored brandy, although Napoleon had made things difficult in that regard.

Having put off meeting these cousins long enough, he took the stairs down to the drawing room.

Three strapping young men in Highland garb turned their heads as he entered. He could tell in an instant what they thought of his formal attire. He suddenly felt ridiculous.

"Tavish," the tallest brother said, offering his hand. "Ye must be Cousin Kenneth."

There was no attempt to recognize the ducal title. To this bright-eyed young man who dwarfed him, he was simply a cousin. "Indeed," he replied, accepting Tavish's bone-crushing handshake. "And these are your brothers."

"Aye, Payton and Niven."

The brothers shook his hand with the same vise-like grip.

An elderly man rose from the settee. "By 'eck, Maureen must be proud o' ye," he said. "I'm yer Uncle Gregor."

Kenneth was startled by the realization that this visit might not turn out how he expected when his long-lost uncle embraced him and thumped him heartily on the back. It was an expression of genuine affection that brought a lump to his throat.

∼

Seated in her mother's parlor at the Dower House, Lady Daisy Hawkins fidgeted with the lace cuffs of her gown. She couldn't deny she was looking forward to meeting Scottish cousins for the first time. She'd heard their earlier arrival at the main house. Life had become rather predictable since the death of her father. Kenneth took his responsibilities as duke very seriously. She rarely saw her brother and sometimes felt she was the lone occupant of the enormous Ramsay House. The place already seemed cozier with male voices echoing. She'd been tempted to seek out her cousins, but had been obliged to submit to her maid's attempts to tame her hair and dress her before she left for the Dower House.

It was difficult to sense her mother's feelings. Seated

on the sofa, Maureen Hawkins gave the impression of being calm and serene—an icy demeanor Daisy had watched her perfect over the years. However, in a few minutes, she would come face to face with a brother who'd shunned her after she left Scotland. Daisy's Uncle Gregor had apparently disapproved of his sister's elopement with an English gentleman.

But this selfsame brother had come cap in hand with his nephews, seeking financial backers for a distillery somewhere in the wilds of Scotland. Daisy had no notion of how whisky was distilled, but the *ton* seemed to have suddenly decided the brew was the fashionable intoxicating liquor to imbibe—simply because Prinny had a taste for it. She had no respect for the Prince Regent's indulgence in all manner of decadent pursuits.

However, she did love her mother, and if these Scottish relatives thought to drag up old resentments, Daisy would have something to say about it. They were probably an ill-mannered lot. Did Highlanders even know how to read?

Her heart thudded in her ears when the parlor door was thrust open and her brother entered with four men. Gray hair and a lined face were the only tell-tale signs that one of them was older. The others—oh, my! She'd never seen shoulders so broad, nor men so tall for that matter. They were a head taller than Kenneth and he was not a small man. Heat flooded her face. She was secretly thrilled the three giants all wore kilts, though why that was she couldn't say. It struck her men's legs were very different from her own.

Tavish's apprehension about the reunion of a brother and sister who hadn't seen each other in thirty years and who'd parted on bad terms—well, it seemed his worries were unfounded.

Aunty Maureen behaved as he supposed a duchess should—with polite decorum and a warm smile. She even allowed Gregor to kiss her hand—a courtesy Tavish had never seen his rough-and-ready uncle offer to any woman before.

"Lass," Gregor rasped. "'Tis good to see ye in fine fettle. I didna ken ye'd lost Freddie to yon grim reaper."

Distress flickered in her eyes for only a moment before she replied. "Yes, eighteen months ago. Now, introduce me to these strapping gentlemen I assume are my nephews."

Gregor suddenly paled, seemingly at a loss. Tavish stepped forward and took her hand. "I'm Tavish King, Aunty," he said. "Walter's eldest son."

"Yes," she replied, shaking his hand with a surprisingly firm grip. "You've a look of him, though I doubt you have his temper."

"Ye kent my Da, then?" he quipped, relieved she hadn't expected him to kiss her knuckles.

"Aye," she replied with a chuckle. "I ne'er understood what my sister saw in him."

Encouraged by her lapse into the brogue, he gestured to his brothers. "Payton and Niven," he explained.

"Aunty," they chorused as she shook hands with them.

"You've already met Kenneth at the main house," she said. "Now, I'll introduce Lady Daisy Hawkins, my daughter."

She took the elbow of the young woman who'd been staring at their kilts since they entered.

Unsure how people in London greeted relatives of their own generation they didn't know they had, Tavish decided to act as he would have in Glengeárr. He took her hand, drew her into an embrace and kissed her cheek. "Cousin Daisy," he said, a little alarmed by her pallor. Payton and Niven followed his example.

She swayed. For a moment, he feared she might swoon. Then she rallied. "Cousins," she said. "It's a pleasure to meet you."

Upon first learning he had a female cousin, Tavish had entertained notions that the search for a bride might be easier than he anticipated. The raven-haired Daisy Hawkins was certainly beautiful and well endowed in all the right female places. She probably had friends who were equally attractive. However, as they settled into the comfortable chairs in the parlor, she seemed unable to take her eyes off Payton's kilt. He'd have to have a word with his brother about sitting in polite company with his knees spread apart and his socks around his ankles.

DINNER

The dinner progressed more smoothly than Kenneth expected. Tavish brandished a bottle of whisky upon first arriving. "A wee dram to sample," he declared, frowning when the butler took it from him.

"He'll put it in the library, for later," Kenneth explained.

For two people who'd been estranged for thirty years, his mother and uncle seemed to get along fine, although he sensed the older man was controlling his tongue. The three cousins exchanged puzzled frowns whenever Gregor uttered some harmless observation.

They, on the other hand, quickly became the life and soul of the evening. Not reticent about voicing opinions, they laughed heartily and tucked into the food like starving children.

It was behavior many of Kenneth's associates would deem *coarse*, but he found it refreshingly natural.

As for his sister, he'd never seen Daisy so animated.

She grilled the middle brother about every facet of whisky distillation, much to the annoyance of Tavish King.

Then his mother brought up the topic of the ball. "It will provide an opportunity for you to meet people who might be useful to your purpose."

The brothers suddenly stopped talking.

Gregor came to their rescue. "Ye hafta understand, the lads dinna attend balls in Glengeárr. Dances, aye, with fiddlers who play reels, strathspeys and the like. Ye remember, Maureen?"

Kenneth had a fleeting vision of his burly cousins dancing a reel at the ball. Kilts awhirl. However, he controlled the urge to laugh out loud when he saw wistful tears welling in his mother's eyes.

It struck him like a blow to the belly he'd never given a thought to the life his mother had left behind in Scotland. Scottish blood ran in his veins, yet he'd always considered himself thoroughly English. His mother had never uttered a word about his total lack of sensitivity to her feelings. He'd assumed she'd been anxious to leave her family and her country behind. He'd been blind.

"Perhaps we can prevail upon our cousins to demonstrate a reel at the ball," he suggested, worried he'd gone too far when the Highlanders gaped.

"What a wonderful idea," Daisy exclaimed.

"Aye," Gregor and his estranged sister agreed enthusiastically.

∾

"I CAN SEE you men are impatient to be off to enjoy your port and cigars," Aunty Maureen declared after the meal.

Tavish was aware of this custom, but why indulge in a glass of port when a fine single malt awaited them in the library?

"We were limited to fourteen pounds o' luggage each," he explained. "But we managed to smuggle a crate o' *Uachdaran* aboard yon mail coach," he reminded Kenneth, relieved when his cousin grinned.

A few minutes later, Payton, Niven and Gregor were settled in comfortable red leather chairs in the library. They declined the offer of cigars.

Puffing on his cigar, Kenneth soon had five glasses ready for Tavish to fill. "I'm looking forward to this," he gushed, rubbing his hands together.

"*Slàinte*," Gregor said, raising his glass.

The brothers echoed the toast.

"Here's mud in your eye," Kenneth replied, sipping the amber liquid.

Confident though they were of the quality of their whisky, the Kings nevertheless held their breath as they waited for a reaction. There was no guarantee Kenneth would appreciate the genuine article. Englishmen were reputed to favor brandy.

Tavish's hopes faltered when his cousin closed his eyes before taking another sip.

Suddenly, Kenneth's eyes were as wide as saucers. "Dash my wig and trouser buttons," he exclaimed.

Since his cousin was grinning from ear to ear, Tavish took this peculiar sentiment to mean he liked the whisky, though what a wig had to do with it...

Relief surged when it was Kenneth who insisted on another "wee dram". Maybe this Sassenach cousin was the son of a Scot after all!

∼

"Come along, Daisy," Maureen declared. "Let's see what the ruckus is about. Why should the men have all the fun?"

Her daughter's startled reaction didn't come as a surprise. For thirty years, Maureen had played the part of the dutiful wife of an English nobleman. She'd slipped effortlessly into the demanding role of duchess when Freddie unexpectedly inherited a dukedom.

She done it all happily—but at what cost to her true self?

Seeing Gregor again and enjoying her nephews' brogue and down-to-earth Highland candor had resurrected feelings she thought long dead and buried. The Scot in her wanted a taste of that fine single malt whisky.

"We shouldn't interrupt," Daisy said. "You know how men are."

The hint of fear in her daughter's voice saddened Maureen. The spunky lass who'd grown up in Glengeárr and eloped with a Sassenach had failed Daisy. "Just because men rule the world doesna mean we hafta do everything they expect o' us."

"I'm not sure what's come over you, Mother," Daisy began.

"A hankering for a wee dram, my lassie," she replied.

Daisy couldn't say what was considered so marvelous about the taste of Scotch whisky. She accepted a glass of the stuff when her mother insisted and sipped politely, reluctant to admit she didn't care for it at all. Had it not been for an unladylike urge to have Payton King keep smiling in response to everything she said, she might have grimaced when the fiery liquid burned her throat.

The bottle was almost empty when Uncle Gregor burst into song. She didn't understand a word of whatever language it was but, apparently, Maureen Hawkins did. Daisy had never heard her mother sing, let alone belt out the lyrics of some Highland ballad, all the while raising her empty glass in a mock toast to her nephews.

They, of course, all had wonderful singing voices. Payton in particular was gifted with a melodious baritone that struck a chord deep in Daisy's abdomen.

She'd thought the ballad was a lament, but even Kenneth, who had hummed along, seemed incapable of controlling his laughter when the song came to an end.

"Perhaps we should be getting back to the main house," she suggested, feeling like the odd one out. "It's late."

More hysterical laughter greeted this announcement.

"I'll get the...er...carriage...brought round," her brother finally said between hiccups.

The Kings heaved their bulk out of the red chairs with surprising agility. They'd drunk as much as everyone else but perhaps they were more used to strong liquor.

"I reckon we'll walk," Tavish said. "'Tisna far and the night air will do us good."

"I'll walk with you," Kenneth said.

Disappointed she wouldn't be sharing the short carriage ride with Payton King, Daisy watched in amazement as her mother embraced each of her Scottish guests in turn and bade them goodnight.

A teary-eyed Gregor decided he was too unsteady on his feet to walk, so his nephews left without him.

Five minutes later, Daisy and Uncle Gregor were in the carriage on the way to the main house.

"My cousins seem to enjoy life," she remarked when they rode past the singing quartet.

"Aye," Gregor agreed. "Maybe they've realized getting hitched willna be so bad."

"Hitched?" she asked.

"Aye. We came to London in search o' wealthy brides for the lads."

A chill stole up her spine. "Wealthy?" she murmured.

"Yon distillery needs cash."

Sinking back against the squabs, she folded her arms. She thought she'd seen genuine interest in Payton's flirtatious smiles but obviously the King brothers were only interested in securing hefty dowries.

Mixed Emotions

"I've had a wonderful idea," Kenneth enthused the following morning at breakfast.

His mother pinched the bridge of her nose. "Must you speak so loudly?"

He toyed with the notion of teasing her about drinking too much whisky the previous evening, but then thought better of it. He'd actually enjoyed seeing his normally straitlaced mother let down her guard. Perhaps he'd been allowed a glimpse of the real person behind the stoic mask she'd worn since he was a child. He suspected he might like this new side of his mother.

Daisy scowled. "What's your marvelous idea?"

His sister's mood was puzzling and couldn't be attributed to over-imbibing. She'd barely touched a drop of Scotch. Was that the problem? A wee dram or two might loosen up his overly serious sister. She'd definitely flirted with one of the Kings yesterday. Today, the sullen sister was back. Undaunted by her sulk, he soldiered on.

"I thought we could host practice sessions for the Highland reel demonstration that I proposed."

His mother's eyes brightened. "What did you have in mind?"

"I'm sure our Highlander cousins don't need to practice dancing a reel," Daisy retorted sarcastically.

Still not sure what had got her back up, he counted to ten before replying. "No, but I'd like to join in, just to make our visitors feel more at ease."

His mother nodded. "Me too. I havena danced a reel since…"

She seemed lost in thoughts of the past. Seeking to rescue her from a bout of maudlin tears, he suggested, "We need more females to join in."

"Count me out," Daisy exclaimed.

Annoyed, Kenneth decided to assert his authority. What was the use of being a duke if he couldn't convince his own sister? "No, I intend to invite Priscilla Graham. She'll only be allowed to come if I inform her parents you'll be present."

The brilliant plan to invite the woman he was wooing had come to him during the night. All things Scottish seemed to appeal to her. Socializing informally with his family would perhaps open her eyes to the life she could have if she married him.

"Aye, yes," his mother gushed. "Lovely girl. You'll enjoy her company, Daisy."

A worry niggled at the back of his mind. He foresaw a flaw in the plan if his mother got too close to the whisky.

"I THOUGHT you'd be excited, Miss Piper," Molly said as she settled the bonnet on her mistress' head.

"I am," Piper replied, lifting her chin so her maid could tie the ribbons. "Just nervous, I suppose."

"Well," Molly persisted. "I'm looking forward to watching when I accompany you. Never seen a Scottish dance."

"It's actually not difficult. I learned quickly when I visited Grandad Jock in Scotland. Scottish dances are a lot of fun. Scots tend to throw themselves into the spirit of the dance, especially if there's a talented fiddler playing. People here are overly worried about keeping up appearances and the music is too slow. No, I'm apprehensive about the duke's reason for inviting me to the rehearsals."

"You don't sound very thrilled about his wooing."

Piper couldn't seem to make her mother understand her feelings, but Molly had been her lady's maid for many years. She'd been made privy to all there was to know about the garrulous Molly and her various beaux. Perhaps the maid would understand the desire for passion in a marriage.

"Well, I can tell you," Molly began before Piper had a chance to speak. "If I'd a duke pursuing me, I'd drag him to the altar before you could say *My Giddy Aunt*."

So much for confiding in Molly. Piper might have known her promiscuous servant didn't hanker for passion and true love.

Snorting horses in the avenue drew the maid's attention to the window. "Your carriage awaits, Your Ladyship," she declared with a grin.

They descended the stairs to the foyer where her nervous mother waited to see her off. "Remember what your father and I discussed," she warned.

More confused than ever about her father's intentions with regard to her happiness, Piper kissed her mother's cheek, nodded to Higgins holding open the door and allowed James Footman to help her mount the steps of the Hawkins ducal carriage.

"I just hope these Highlanders are light on their feet," she told Molly as the vehicle lurched forward. "I don't fancy a big booted foot landing on my wee toes."

Her maid's hearty laughter helped dispel some of her anxiety about the afternoon's activity.

∽

Tavish had mixed feelings about the gathering. The ballroom was intimidatingly enormous. It must have taken an army of servants to light the dozens of crystal chandeliers. Aunty Maureen assured him it wouldn't seem so big once it was full of people. Try as he might, he couldn't imagine it. The prospect of dancing a reel with hundreds of strangers watching held no appeal, especially since there'd likely be few Scots in the audience. He'd be too worried about making a good impression to immerse himself in the dance.

At least suitable music had been taken care of. Kenneth produced a violin from the Music Room. It hadn't been played in many a year, but Niven was a talented fiddle player who could make any instrument sing.

Speaking of his cousin—Kenneth's attention was fixed on the entry doors.

"The rehearsal was yer son's idea," he said to his aunty. "But he seems distracted."

"Waiting for his lady love," she replied.

"He's betrothed?" he asked.

"More or less," she replied cryptically. "Priscilla Graham's a lovely girl. You'll like her."

Tavish wasn't proud of his initial reaction to the woman's name. "Sounds very English," he muttered under his breath, anticipating the arrival of some stuck-up debutante.

He decided against questioning his aunty about Daisy's sullen demeanor. Payton greeted his cousin warmly when she arrived and started explaining a few of the steps. She gave him the cold shoulder and walked away.

"Who can understand Sassenachs?" his brother muttered in response to the unspoken question in Tavish's eyes.

"Aye," Gregor agreed with a sigh.

Tavish couldn't rid himself of the vague suspicion that something had gone on in the carriage the previous evening. His uncle wasn't known for his discretion, especially after a few drams of whisky.

He was distracted when Kenneth rushed out of the ballroom, no doubt to greet his lass.

Tavish's mind went completely blank when his cousin returned a few minutes later, a stunningly beautiful goddess on his arm.

The rampant sexual urges of his youth had faded in

his twenties. He was embarrassed and ashamed when his cock sprang to life and heartily saluted his cousin's betrothed.

REELING

Peculiar things happened to Piper when she set eyes on the tall Highlander staring at her with his mouth agape.

Her knees threatened to buckle. She broke out in a most unladylike sweat. Her nipples tingled and she was seized by an urge to thrust out breasts she'd always feared were too big for her slender frame. Shaking, she was torn between laughing out loud and bursting into tears.

"Are you unwell, my dear?" Kenneth asked.

It came to her she had a death grip on his arm—a tactic born of the desperation to stay upright. "Quite well," she replied hoarsely.

"No need to be nervous," he assured her. "My cousins are easy going chaps. Highlanders, you know."

Piper did not need to be told the kilted giant striding toward her was a Highlander. Nor did the fire in his eyes bespeak an easy going nature. *Chap* didn't do him justice. This cousin was a man in every sense of the word.

"Miss Graham," Kenneth declared. "I'm pleased to introduce Tavish King."

"Mr. King," she replied, trembling when the visitor took hold of her hand and brushed a courtly kiss on her knuckles.

"Please, my name is Tavish," he rumbled. "Mr. King was my father."

Unable to take her eyes off his massive hand and mortified by the moisture gushing from a very intimate place, she closed her eyes and let his unusual name thrum through her. "And I'm Piper," she murmured.

"Piper?" he asked. "I thought…"

Kenneth's bristling broke the spell. "Miss Graham's given name is Priscilla," he growled. "However…"

"I prefer Piper," the Scot declared with a saucy grin.

∼

His cousin's betrothed was not what Tavish nor his unruly cock had expected. He couldn't remember the last time he'd experienced such a hard-on. He seemed unable to let go of her hand, though he wished she would remove her gloves. Perhaps if he peeled them off…

Kenneth's loud cough jolted him to his senses. Tavish was shaming himself and his family by flirting with Miss Graham. She belonged to his cousin.

A vision of Kenneth and the lass cavorting in bed together gave rise to a dizzying rage. She clearly loved the man if the unmistakable aroma of female arousal was any indication.

He toyed with the idea of fleeing the ballroom, but that would be the act of a coward.

Everyone shuffled apart when Gregor's voice penetrated the fog. "I'll explain how this works. We'll be doing an Eightsome Reel."

"We're short one lass, Uncle," Niven pointed out.

The maid who'd followed Miss Graham into the ballroom coughed loudly.

"Aye, ye'll do, lass," Gregor announced, beckoning the servant to join the group.

Kenneth clenched his jaw as the maid came forward.

Miss Graham smiled at her servant.

"Now, the first Eightsome of any gatherin' is usually a 'Kilted Eightsome' which means only kilted gentlemen are allowed on the dance floor," Gregor explained with gravity.

"I hardly think that pertains here," Aunty Maureen said with a hint of sarcasm.

"I certainly won't be wearing a kilt," Kenneth added, earning a pouting glare from his fiancée.

Daisy snorted.

Gregor ignored them all. "Everyone choose a partner," he instructed.

"Miss Graham and I will be partners," Kenneth declared.

She pouted but allowed him to take her hand.

"I'll partner Miss Hawkins," Payton said.

"Sorry," Kenneth's sister replied, moving to stand next to Tavish. "I'll dance with your older brother."

"I suggest Payton partner my sister," Gregor said, coming to his fuming nephew's rescue.

"We've a problem if I'm to play the fiddle," Niven said, also sensing Payton's annoyance. "I canna dance and play at the same time."

"Aye," Gregor agreed, scraping fingernails through his whiskers. "We dinna need the music until we've learned the steps."

"Harrison can take your place," Kenneth suggested, turning to the maid. "Go fetch him so he can watch and learn," he commanded with a dismissive wave.

The maid's glower tightened Tavish's gut. The thought of the very proper English butler kicking up his heels bordered on the comical. However, none of the Kings would ever speak in such a demeaning manner to an employee, not even the lad who swept the floor of the distillery.

"In that case, I'll partner Miss Graham's maidservant," Niven said. "What's yer name, lass?"

"Molly, Sir," she replied with a seductive smile.

"If ye please, see if ye can find yon butler, Molly," Niven said.

Tavish was proud of the way Niven had subtly demonstrated how to treat the servant with respect.

"Now, form a circle and hold hands," Gregor commanded. "Ladies to the right o' your partners." He pointed to Tavish. "Ye ken the steps, so ye and Miss Daisy are couple number one, Payton and his aunty are number two, Kenneth and his fiancée number three, Niven and Molly number four.

"Now, the circle goes round clockwise eight steps, then t'other way eight steps. Let's try that first then we'll have a go at the teapot and the grand chain."

Twenty excruciating minutes later, Gregor suggested they take a break. "What ails ye, laddie?" he growled close to Tavish's ear.

Tavish had no answer. As the dancing lesson progressed, it was as though he suddenly didn't know his left from his right, clockwise from counterclockwise. He trod on Daisy's toes so many times, he feared she'd walk with a permanent limp. The more he apologized, the more she pouted. When the butler finally took Niven's place and his brother struck up the fiddle, Tavish couldn't get his feet to move in time with the music.

"A *mon* would think ye'd ne'er danced a reel before," Gregor muttered. "Yon butler is faring better than ye."

"Is it hot in here?" Tavish replied, worried he'd come into contact with some noxious disease in the course of their travels.

Red in the face after what Tavish suspected was unusual exertion, Kenneth slapped him on the back. "Hate to mention it, old chap," he panted with a grin. "Miss Graham and I are putting you to shame."

Therein lay Tavish's torment. Piper Graham danced a reel as well as any Highland lass. She even made Kenneth look like he knew what he was doing.

～

Piper accepted it was naughty, but she kept wishing Tavish King's swishing kilt would ride up just a tiny bit more as the dancing progressed. Her Scottish grandfather often jested that a Scotsman went *bare-arsed* under his kilt, but she'd always wondered. And those well-muscled legs!

However, for a Scot, he seemed oddly unfamiliar with the sequence of a reel. His clenched jaw indicated he wasn't enjoying himself. Mind you, the sulking Daisy Hawkins was obviously determined not to have fun, or perhaps the long journey had taken a lot out of the visitors. Payton and Niven's exuberance gave the lie to that theory.

Kenneth was slowly getting the hang of the dance. Had she not wrestled him into the correct position several times, they'd have spoiled the whole set. She had to admit that he was very handsome when he laughed. He'd looked so stern when the rehearsal began, but the rousing beat soon worked its magic.

As for his mother, she whooped and yelled, clearly under the spell of Niven King's prowess with the fiddle. Piper had not lent much credence to Kenneth's assertion his very proper English mother was originally from Scotland, but here was the proof.

Caught up in the heart-stopping music, Piper also found herself transported back to happy times spent with her grandfather in Galloway.

If her parents persisted in forcing a marriage with Kenneth Hawkins, she could perhaps flee to the Lowlands. Grandad Jock would welcome her with open arms.

THE PITCH

S till reeling from his embarrassing performance at the previous day's dance rehearsal, Tavish tried to ignore his brothers' jibes as they prepared for a meeting with Kenneth's man of business.

He hadn't slept well, his disturbing dreams haunted by Piper Graham. What was it about the lass that had his gut tied in knots and his manhood on permanent salute?

"Do ye feel more like yerself this morn?" Payton asked.

"Do ye think Daisy can walk today or do ye suppose ye did permanent damage?" Niven teased.

"Verra funny," Tavish retorted. "I just didna feel like dancin'. What's amiss wi' that?"

He bristled when Gregor entered without knocking. "That lass is promised to yer cousin, ye ken?" his uncle declared.

He might have known his perceptive relative would discern the reason for his distraction.

"Hah!" Payton exclaimed. "Ye've the hots fer yon Piper."

"Aye. A bonnie lass can turn a *mon* into a clumsy ass every time," Niven chirped.

"Look," Tavish growled, anxious to shift the conversation elsewhere. "We came here to promote our whisky."

"And to find wives," Gregor reminded him.

Tavish had heard enough. "Miss Graham canna wed any one of us. She's in love with Kenneth, and that's an end to it."

"Dinna be so sure," Gregor replied.

A light tapping at the door prevented Tavish from demanding to know exactly what his uncle meant by that cryptic remark.

"His Grace awaits you in his study, gentlemen," a male voice called.

There was no more ribaldry as they straightened plaids, pulled up socks, donned berets, and secured clan brooches.

"Aye, ye'll do, my braw Highland laddies," Gregor declared, hoisting aloft a bottle of *Uachdaran*. "Yon Sassenach will be gobsmacked."

"Wish I'd brought my bagpipes," Niven muttered as they marched out of the chamber.

∼

KENNETH HAD to stifle a smile when his Scottish cousins entered his study. The only thing missing from the impressive display was a set of bagpipes. His man of business gaped, clearly awed.

Kenneth had a momentary notion to ask his relatives where he might procure his own kilt, but quickly dismissed the notion as fanciful. He considered himself fit but admitted he didn't have the same well-muscled legs as the King brothers.

"Gentlemen," he declared. "May I present Richard Mainwaring, my man of business."

Tavish extended a hand. "Tavish King," he said. "Pleased to meet ye. These are my bothers, Payton and Niven and my uncle, Gregor."

For years, Kenneth's father had depended on Mainwaring's serious demeanor and unerring judgment. As he shook hands with the Scots, the man blushed like a coy maiden.

"His Grace has been enthusiastic about the superior quality of your whisky," Mainwaring gushed, eyeing the bottle in Gregor's hand.

Gregor didn't hesitate. "Ye've glasses to hand, nephew?" he asked, pulling out the stopper. "'Tis ne'er too early in the day to enjoy a wee dram."

"Of course," Kenneth replied, gesturing to a nearby tray. Did his uncle think he'd be unprepared?

Gregor poured while Tavish explained some of the practices that made their whisky superior.

"We're one of only a handful of distilleries to still turn our malt by hand. It's hard work, but the end justifies the means."

"Can you explain that in more detail?" Kenneth asked.

"When barley is malting, it generates a lot o' heat, so we turn it by hand, every eight hours, seven days a week, to keep the air flowin' and introduce exactly the right amount o' moisture to absorb the reek."

"Reek?" Mainwaring asked, holding his glass up to the light.

"The aromatic smoke produced by the peat smoldering in our kilns," Tavish explained.

"You burn peat, not wood or coal?" Mainwaring asked.

"Aye. We gather it from the moor."

"You might not dance well, Cousin," Kenneth jested, coming to the realization there was more to distilling whisky than he'd imagined. "But you certainly know your stuff."

He'd intended the jibe as a compliment, but Tavish scowled. He wondered again what had caused his capable cousin to develop two left feet at the rehearsal.

~

As he explained the day-to-day process of distilling, Tavish's confidence returned. Whisky was his passion and he intended to make sure this Mainwaring chap understood that.

"The peat from Glengeárr moor is vitally important to the unique flavor and character of our whisky. The moor lies just seven miles from our distillery and its peat is over nine thousand years old in places and up to ten feet deep. 'Tis rich in fragrant heather from the top layer of *fogg* to the densely compacted *yarphie* and finally the ancient moss. Once a year, we carefully hand-cut peat and dry it naturally before burning it in our kilns. Its aromatic smoke infuses the malting barley."

Mainwaring had been sipping the dram, his eyes widening with every sip. "This is outstanding," he declared. "And your relatives clearly know what they are about, Your Grace. I'd say it's an endeavor deserving of investment."

Tavish exchanged a confused glance with his brothers. They hadn't considered any other means of securing funds besides marriage. Perhaps they could return to Scotland as carefree bachelors. Strangely, the prospect didn't sit well in Tavish's gut.

Kenneth narrowed his eyes. "Tell us your thoughts on the future of your business," he said gruffly.

Tavish's affable cousin had suddenly transformed into a shrewd investor. "We want to age our whisky in barrels that have previously been used to age sherry."

"In Spain," Gregor explained in answer to Kenneth's puzzled frown. "So we hafta get them shipped back to us."

"Shipped back?"

"Aye. We made the staves using methods pioneered by our Viking ancestors so liquid canna seep out. Then we shipped them to Spain where they were made into barrels which have been used to age sherry for three years. Now, we want to get them back. That was the agreement with the Spaniards."

"Sounds like a long process," Kenneth observed.

"Distilling fine whisky is all about time and patience, Cousin," Tavish replied confidently.

TWISTING IN THE WIND

"One of the Kings is taken with you, Miss," Molly asserted as she tightened the laces of her mistress' corset. "As you well know."

"I'm sure you're mistaken," Piper replied, not looking forward to another grilling over breakfast. During dinner the previous evening, her mother had harangued her for details of the afternoon's rehearsal. It had been difficult not to keep mentioning one appealing Highlander in particular.

"Why do you suppose the man kept tripping over his own feet?" Molly persisted.

Piper had wondered the same thing. Tavish's uncle had obviously been upset with his nephew, which suggested the clumsy behavior was out of character. He also seemed exasperated with himself.

Despite his ungainly performance, she'd been drawn to him, and not just because of the kilt.

"I'd say you were impressed with him too," Molly accused as she helped Piper into the day gown.

"You're too cheeky for a servant," Piper retorted.

"You can't fool me," her maid replied. "I saw the way you thrust out your chest and then couldn't take your eyes off the man's bare legs."

Laughter bubbled in Piper's throat. "I admit I was hoping to catch a glimpse of...well...you know..."

"You're a bad girl, Miss Piper Graham," Molly declared as a fit of giggles seized them both.

It took a few minutes to compose themselves sufficiently to make their way downstairs.

Piper's good humor fled when she espied another bouquet of yellow tea roses on the table in the foyer and the peculiar expression on her mother's face.

"Another drive in the park?" she asked, trying to think of an excuse.

Lady Graham's tight smile was brief. "Yes, but he hopes you don't mind if he brings his cousins along."

∽

TO KENNETH'S SURPRISE, Tavish wasn't enthusiastic about accompanying him and Miss Graham on a ride through Hyde Park. However, Payton and Niven were eager to enjoy the sights and sounds of the famous landmark.

"It will be a chance to meet the Grahams," he assured Tavish. "I'll wager the fellow has a bob or two to invest."

"Piper's family is wealthy?" his cousin asked.

Kenneth had to think about that for a moment. It was a question people in polite society didn't ask. However, the Kings were seeking investors so he supposed it was a legitimate inquiry. He just wished

Tavish would refrain from using his intended's unsuitable nickname. "I don't expect a large dowry," he admitted. "But the family certainly isn't poor."

"Dowry?" Tavish growled.

Kenneth couldn't imagine why that prospect annoyed his cousin. Mayhap dowries weren't the norm in Scotland. "Yes. When Miss Graham and I marry, her family will provide..."

"I ken what a dowry is," Tavish retorted angrily. "So, ye and she are affianced?"

"Yes," he replied, convinced it wasn't a lie in the true sense of the word. Priscilla would eventually come round to accepting his suit. He was a duke after all. "I've already taken the first step towards, shall we say, a more intimate relationship. I've invited her to call me Ramsay."

He became increasingly worried about the wisdom of the afternoon's ride when Tavish clenched his jaw and glared at him as if he had two heads.

∽

"I think ye lads should go on without me," Tavish muttered after Kenneth went ahead.

"Nay," Payton retorted. "We're in this together. We depend on ye to be our spokesperson, our chieftain if ye like."

"Aye," Niven agreed. "Ye dinna want Kenneth touting the merits o' our whisky to Mr. Graham."

"The Duke o' Ramsay, ye mean. Ye must be sure to use his title."

"What's put that bee in yer bonnet?" Payton

demanded.

"Can ye believe our twit of a cousin has invited the woman he plans to marry to call him Ramsay?"

He knew as soon as the words were out of his mouth he'd given himself away.

"And ye care about this because?" Niven asked pointedly.

Tavish could see no way out of the trap he'd set for himself. "A lass like Piper needs a man who can show her what love's all about."

"And that would be ye, I suppose," Payton taunted.

"Weel, I'd want her to call me by my given name, not some bloody title."

Niven fluttered his eyelashes. "Oh, Tavish," he declared in a falsetto voice. "Ye're such a braw laddie."

"Ye dinna have a title in any case," Payton pointed out. "Except the Romeo o' Glengeárr."

Tavish fumed as he watched his brothers fall to their knees laughing. He should have expected his uncle to walk in at that precise moment.

"Are ye nay ready, lads?" Gregor asked. "Kenneth's waitin'."

"Weel, let's go," Payton exclaimed. "We canna keep Ramsay away from his lady love. And it'll be fun watchin' Tavish twist in the wind."

"Wheest," Gregor retorted in response to the laughter. "I'm glad I'm nay comin' with ye lunatics."

"Ye're stayin' here?" Tavish asked.

"Aye. Me and Maureen are plannin' a wee discussion."

That sounded ominous to Tavish.

TOUCHY TOPIC

Piper couldn't recall a more uncomfortable gathering in her parent's drawing room. Her father was clearly delighted to welcome the King brothers. Throughout the obligatory tea ritual, he talked on and on about his childhood in Scotland and asked a multitude of questions about present day happenings in the country of his birth. They discussed tartans, Jacobite rebellions, and the injustices perpetrated on Clan MacGregor when it came to light the Kings were a sept of that clan. Piper had never heard him speak more than a few words at a time. She even detected a trace of a brogue she'd not noticed before. She hadn't previously given a thought to her father's family living through the hell of Culloden's aftermath and the brutalities of religious strife in the Lowlands.

On the other side of the cozy room, Piper's mother grew more and more fidgety as the afternoon progressed. If she'd bitten into a slice of lemon directly from the tea service, she couldn't have looked more sour. The only person she treated with fawning politeness was Kenneth.

It was difficult to gauge the duke's feelings, especially in light of the recent revelation that his mother had also grown up in Scotland. That was perhaps on his mind as he tried half-heartedly to contribute to the conversation. He declined the offer of coffee, much to the dismay of Piper's mother. As a duke, he was used to being the center of attention. Despite Margaret Graham's sterling efforts to the contrary, the King brothers were the stars of the show.

Piper herself became certain of one thing. Her attraction to Tavish King at the rehearsal wasn't a flash in the pan. He'd abandoned the kilt in favor of tartan trews, but still drew her like a lodestone. She even loved the sound of his voice. There was an undeniable alchemy between them.

However, she had to be careful. Her mother and Kenneth must not suspect her feelings. After all, Tavish lived in Scotland. Highlanders were known to hold English people in contempt. She was simply drawn to him because he was an attractive man. And perhaps his Scottishness had something to do with it. She'd always had a weak spot for Scots. Although, Payton and Niven were just as handsome, broad-shouldered and charming as their older brother. Indeed, they were clearly more at ease than Tavish—even while trying to balance teacups. She liked them—they were a refreshing change from the stilted London set—but that was as far as it went.

Then, while she was daydreaming, the conversation

wandered into the risky topic of money. Unlikely as it seemed, the Duke of Ramsay was the person who brought it up.

∼

Tavish supposed he should be grateful to his cousin for bringing up the idea of investment. Heaven knew the proud Scot in him wasn't comfortable doing it. However, as majority owner of the distillery, it was his responsibility.

He was beginning to think the idea of seeking a bride was fraught with too much difficulty. He'd met a woman he wanted, but couldn't have, no matter the insistence of his stubborn cock that she was the one for him. Seeking investment from wealthy patrons was perhaps a better way to go—easier on the heart.

"Mmm," was Graham's response to Kenneth's probing about money. Judging by the sudden pallor, Tavish would guess the man had no coin to invest. Or perhaps he kept tight rein on his purse, like many a canny Scot.

"There's always my dowry," Piper exclaimed.

"Absolutely not," Lady Graham retorted, her teacup tumbling to the carpet when she rose abruptly.

A maid hurried to assist her, but she fled the room in tears.

"You've done it now, my girl," her father said.

Piper fidgeted with the neckline of her gown, glanced briefly at the scowling Kenneth, then stared at Tavish.

He thought perhaps he should say something into

the uncomfortable silence, but Piper beat him to it. "Of course, I meant the funds I'm to receive from Grandad. He set it up so I can spend it on whatever I want once I come of age, or marry."

"I think my father intended for you to entrust it to your husband," Graham said.

"Quite right, Sir," Kenneth replied.

"You have no right to an opinion, Ramsay. We're not married yet," Piper retorted before she too fled the room.

∾

Kenneth wasn't certain how he'd managed to set the cat among the pigeons. He was normally the catalyst for stimulating conversation at tea parties. People always followed his lead. Surely friends could have a discussion about investment without…

Of course! Talk of money had upset the women. He should have known better than to bring up the topic with females present. Every man knew the members of the fairer sex weren't capable of rational thought when it came to money. He'd embarrassed Lady Graham and upset dear Priscilla.

He hadn't known about the inheritance set aside by her Scottish grandfather. Perhaps investing it in the Kings' distillery was a sound idea. He was likely going to put money in. They could be business partners in the endeavor.

"Good grief, man," he whispered under his breath. "Have you lost your senses?"

While they waited for Priscilla's maid to fetch her mistress so they could embark on their ride, he thought maybe he should have a discussion with Graham about the dowry he intended to provide for his daughter.

COOPED UP

Kenneth's barouche was spacious, but Piper felt she was trapped in a small box with four large men and an overly observant maid. When they entered the park, an intermittent drizzle forced the closing of the cover which only added to the discomfort. Conversation was stilted, not surprising given the histrionics of the tea party.

Molly had convinced her to swallow her pride and agree to join the others for the ride. If she were honest with herself, she'd admit spending time with Tavish King was the primary motivation.

Seated across from the long-legged Scot, she was obliged to turn slightly sideways so their feet wouldn't touch. This had the unfortunate result of bringing her skirts into contact with Kenneth's legs since he was seated beside her. Molly's loud throat-clearing indicated she disapproved.

As they passed the Serpentine for the second time,

she was tempted to break free of the web in which she was caught and stretch her legs to touch Tavish's.

Molly might choke!

The situation was beyond ridiculous. Her parents seemed determined to marry her off to a duke for whom she had no amorous feelings. On the other hand, her intimate female parts reacted all too well when she was in Tavish King's presence. He might pretend he wasn't attracted to her, but something in his eyes told her otherwise—not to mention the little red apples that blossomed on his cheeks whenever he was obliged to speak to her. Yet, they were powerless to explore a relationship. She sensed he was too honorable to pursue his cousin's intended. Not that she considered herself Ramsay's intended.

Sticky web indeed.

Offending the Hawkins family could prove financially and socially disastrous for her family if Kenneth decided to be vindictive—doubly ridiculous since she'd made it as clear as she could that she wasn't interested in marrying him. Perhaps it was difficult for a duke to accept he wasn't a maiden's first choice. In that respect, Piper's mother was probably no different from a thousand others anxious for their daughters to marry well.

Piper didn't even know if Tavish King wanted a wife and family. Kenneth was the better bet.

∽

AT HOME IN SCOTLAND, Tavish was used to being in control. Everyone who worked for the Kings deferred to him, even his brothers. Uncle Gregor was the notable exception, but the old man was fond of playing devil's advocate. He usually ended up agreeing with his nephew's decisions.

Tavish King rarely put a foot wrong when it came to distilling whisky.

Dealing with the unexpected complications of life in London was a whole different matter. How was a man supposed to behave when he found himself cooped up in a carriage with a woman he craved but couldn't even approach? The presence of his cousin, two brothers and a judgmental maid didn't help. The effort of keeping his legs from touching Piper's skirts had resulted in his thighs cramping. If he didn't get out and walk it off soon...

Piper's sweet voice penetrated the fog. "The rain has stopped," she said. "Perhaps we could stroll around the Serpentine for a while."

God bless ye, Lass.

Had she sensed his turmoil?

"I suppose we could if we're cautious," Kenneth replied. "Might be wet underfoot."

"'Tis often wet underfoot in the Highlands," Payton quipped. "As a result, Scots are waterproof."

Tavish glanced at Kenneth. If his cousin detected the sarcasm, he gave no sign of it.

The smile in Piper's eyes told him she appreciated the humor.

Kenneth insisted on having the footman wipe down the steps before they could alight. Tavish expected the chuckling Payton to make some comment, but he kept silent.

It felt natural for three braw Scotsmen to reach for the sky and stretch their limbs once they were released from the confines of the carriage. They quickly realized their *faux pas* when Kenneth scowled, Piper gaped and the maid's eyes sparkled.

Piper accepted the offer of Kenneth's arm. Having decided to make the best of the brief respite, Tavish was about to stride off when Piper linked her free arm with his and he was once more reduced to a sweating mass of thwarted male urges.

∽

They hadn't taken a single step before Piper realized her mistake. She should never have touched Tavish King. Now, she had a fiery furnace on one side and a coolly polite gentleman on the other. It was as though some invisible force poured out of the Scot's solid arm into her body.

The urge to press her breast against Tavish's bicep was powerful. Indeed, she wanted to drape herself around his neck and let him carry her. What would his kiss taste like?

Kenneth was a much better conversationalist than his Scottish cousin, but she scarcely heard a word he said. Tavish's terse replies to his cousin's remarks echoed in her womb. The Piper Graham who had no time for men was suddenly a quivering wanton. An independent girl in no hurry to marry thirsted to wrestle Tavish King to the altar.

It was lunacy. He wasn't titled. He lived in Scotland and distilled whisky—a tradesman to all intents and purposes. It was unlikely the production of whisky in a remote part of the Highlands had resulted in great wealth. But she craved him. Wasn't a grand passion what she wanted?

On the short walk back to the carriage and during the return ride to her parents' townhouse, she refused to look at Tavish and mulled over all the sensible reasons to accept Kenneth's suit.

Rejecting him and pursuing Tavish King could prove calamitous for her family, and the Scot might not want her anyway—although the heated glances he sent her way said otherwise.

By the time Kenneth escorted her into her parents' house, she had become convinced of the merits of playing it safe. She would simply bid a polite goodbye to the trio of Scots tagging along behind. Tavish was a passing fancy.

She startled when a beloved voice she hadn't heard for more than a year called her name.

"Piper, lass."

"Grandad!" she squealed, inhaling the familiar aromas of heather and peat smoke as she threw herself into Jock Graham's hearty embrace.

HEART-TO-HEART

Seated in the most comfortable armchair the Dower House possessed, Maureen Hawkins studied the squirming brother who'd disowned her thirty years ago. He'd aged, of course, but was still a handsome rogue and just as opinionated. However, they were in her domain now, and her restless sibling clearly didn't feel at ease in a London withdrawing room. She'd had years to learn the politics of control. "So, Gregor," she said. "Let's be honest with each other."

"Ye ken I dinna have a dishonest bone in my body," he replied, his thumb worrying a bit of frayed binding on the sofa's arm.

It would be a mistake to embark on a back and forth tennis match with that ambiguous statement, so Maureen stuck to the plan. "Tell me about my sister's distillery."

"Ye'll have Walter turning o'er in his grave wi' that question."

"You know as well as I do that our sister was the

reason the enterprise didn't fail the first year after they inherited the business."

"Aye, true enough," he conceded. "And her sons have her gumption and her love o' the business."

"And the knack of making fine whisky."

"Aye, *Uachdaran* is the result of Tavish's creative experiments and his brothers' dedication to the craft."

"And do you think their plans for the future are sound?"

"I wouldna be here if I didna think so," he replied.

"No, I don't suppose it was easy to swallow your pride and seek my help."

Smugly satisfied she'd backed him into a corner, her confidence faltered when he clenched his jaw and stared at her through narrowed eyes. "I'd walk on hot coals to help those lads," he growled. "E'en come a-knockin' for yer forgiveness, Maureen."

It wasn't the abject apology she would have preferred, but it was all she was likely to get. "We all made mistakes back then," she allowed.

"Aye, but ye ended up a duchess and I'm still…"

She held up her hand to silence him. A Gregor who thought less of himself wasn't what she wanted. "None of that. I suspect you've been more of a father to those boys than Walter ever was."

"Aye, I suppose they are my lads in a way. 'Tis the reason I suggested they come to London to find brides. We need to think o' the future o' the distillery."

Maureen struggled to understand. "Surely there are bonny lasses in the glen who can bear bairns."

"Aye, but I'm speaking o' coin, nay bairns. London's

where my nephews will find women with generous dowries."

Maureen had only met her late sister's sons a few days ago, but they didn't strike her as mercenary men who would marry for the sake of money. They were too straightforward and honorable. Tavish certainly hadn't been able to hide his attraction to Priscilla Graham at the rehearsal. It was painfully obvious there was no spark of passion between Kenneth and the Graham girl. Her son might scoff if she spoke to him of the importance of love in a marital relationship, but a loveless marriage had apparently turned her sister into a shrew. Kenneth was a kind and generous man who deserved a wife who loved him.

But Maureen resolved to keep her powder dry and let things take their course in the hope her son wouldn't get his heart broken.

∽

FOR THIRTY YEARS, Gregor had deeply regretted his selfish reaction to his sister's falling in love. He'd often thought to make amends, but as time went on, it became more difficult, then impossible—until his nephews unwittingly provided him with an excuse to travel south.

But pride was an insidious thing. Here was the opportunity to offer a sincere apology but, ornery so-and-so that he was, the proper words stuck in his craw and came out half-hearted.

Determined to confess what he'd wanted to say for thirty years, he clenched his fists and gritted his teeth. "I had no right to judge ye, Maureen. If I'd been less of a tyrant, ye'd mayhap ha'e wed Freddie in Scotland. I suppose I was jealous o' the two o' ye."

His sister's gobsmacked stare didn't come as a surprise. The tears trickling down her cheeks did. "Oh, Gregor," she sighed. "So many wasted years."

"My fault," he admitted, moving to sit beside her. "Too stubborn by far."

She leaned into him when he put an arm around her shoulders. "It's a family trait," she replied. "Moira was bound and determined to wed Walter in spite of our warnings, and I wasn't going to be talked out of marrying Freddie."

"But ye and Freddie loved each other," he said. "I kent it and still tried to deter ye."

Her willingness to cry on his shoulder was humbling. He didn't deserve her forgiveness.

The minutes ticked by until she asked, "Are you sure you want our nephews to marry for money?"

The question caught him off guard. "They need coin if they're to realize all their plans," he replied. "But I dinna want to see them unhappy."

"I haven't known them long, but I suspect those boys are scared to death of following in their parents' footsteps."

"Aye," he agreed with a heavy heart. "Fool that I am, that's exactly what I encouraged them to do."

FEELINGS

Elated her grandfather had come to visit, Piper was nevertheless aware of her mother's disapproving glare. However, elation overcame common sense. "I can't believe you're here," she told her grandfather as she pulled him into the drawing room and beckoned Kenneth and his cousins to follow. "You must meet the Kings, fellow Scotsmen who own and operate a distillery."

"Indeed?" he replied, extending a hand. "Jock Graham."

Tavish accepted the handshake and introduced himself and his brothers. "We're from Glengeárr," he explained.

"Highlanders who distill whisky," her grandfather exclaimed. "Now, there's a surprise!"

He'd made the comment with a twinkle in his eyes, but Piper felt obliged to defend the Kings. "*Uachdaran* is apparently very fine whisky. They've come to London seeking investors, and I was thinking..."

"Piper!" her mother interjected. "You haven't introduced His Grace."

A quick glance at Ramsay bore out her appalling lack of manners. His scowl indicated his annoyance at being overlooked. "I do apologize, Your Grace. Grandfather, may I introduce the Duke of Ramsay, er, a friend of the family, and...er...the Kings' cousin."

She'd succeeded in compounding the insult. She couldn't have made it clearer that she felt more at ease with Tavish and his brothers than with the man who was wooing her. Jock Graham would notice.

"An honor, Yer Grace," her grandfather replied, shaking Ramsay's hand. "*Uachdaran's* well known in Scotland. Have ye an interest in this distillery?"

Apparently sensing Ramsay's discomfort at being snubbed, Tavish stepped in. "My cousin has graciously offered to host us in London," he explained. "His mother is our aunty."

"Shall we be seated?" Piper's mother suggested, her voice an octave higher than normal. "I'll ring for tea."

"Tea?" Jock exclaimed. "Nay, Margaret, not when there's *Uachdaran* to be had. Your home's nearby, I take it, Ramsay? We can adjourn there and these fine lads can tell me all about their distillery."

∾

TAVISH WASN'T surprised Piper wanted to travel the short distance with her grandfather, and that she agreed with Jock's suggestion the Kings accompany them in the Graham carriage. However, he anticipated his cousin would be annoyed. Kenneth had been obliged to transport the fuming Lady Graham in his barouche.

Tavish was puzzled by Piper's aloofness toward Kenneth. She'd paid more attention to him than to her fiancé. Or perhaps it was just the distillery she found so interesting. He didn't perceive her oversight as a deliberate insult to Kenneth. She didn't seem the type. She had, after all, been somewhat over-excited by Jock Graham's arrival. His advent had brought out the more exuberant side of his granddaughter.

She was even more attractive when she blushed. Tavish idly wondered if the blush spread to her glorious breasts.

The Graham conveyance wasn't as spacious as the barouche. Piper had insisted on sitting between her grandfather and Tavish. Seated opposite, Payton and Niven were clearly enjoying their brother's discomfort. The fitted trews made it impossible to conceal his arousal and Tavish could scarcely do anything to rearrange his male parts in the confined space.

The friction of Piper's hip against him was physically arousing, but Tavish came to the realization he was attracted to other things about her. He loved the sound of her voice, her genuine laughter, her personality. Just being with her felt right. In a few short days, she'd become an important part of his life.

Bitter memories of his parents' marriage had always tainted his feelings about the institution. The prospect held no appeal—until he met Piper. She might be a Sassenach, but she was proud of the Scottish blood in her veins. He sensed he could be happy with her as his life partner. But would she want to move to Scotland and help run a distillery? Life in the Highlands was a far cry from the hustle and bustle of London.

More importantly, his uncle's original plan was to secure a wealthy wife who could contribute much needed funds. Gregor deemed love unimportant, but he'd never been married. Piper had mentioned money from her grandfather, but Jock Graham might not agree and her parents certainly wouldn't.

Then there was the added problem of Kenneth, though Tavish was beginning to sense there was no formal agreement in place between the Hawkins and the Grahams concerning a marriage.

Just what was the relationship between Piper and Kenneth?

For that matter, exactly what was it Tavish felt for Piper? He'd never been in love, and this overwhelming physical and emotional craving for a woman was new.

∼

PIPER KNEW there'd be a price to pay. Her mother would be livid. She'd never liked Jock Graham and disapproved of Piper's love for her grandfather. The reasons remained a perplexing mystery.

Ramsay had a right to be upset. She'd failed to treat him with the respect his title merited.

Meeting Tavish King had made it clear to her that she could never marry Kenneth Hawkins. Simply sitting next to the Scot ignited cravings in intimate parts of her body. She wanted him physically, but she also enjoyed his company. He was genuine, honorable and proud of his accomplishments, not to mention easy on the eye!

Her parents would decry his lack of a title; her mother might faint dead away if she married a Scot.

But she was getting ahead of herself. Tavish might not feel the same overwhelming need to be with her.

Piper had to put things right. Jock Graham would support whatever decision she made. It was risky, and not behavior befitting a lady, but she had to somehow ascertain how Tavish felt about her.

A Happy Gathering

Kenneth was relieved to finally be rid of Lady Graham when they reached Ramsay House. The woman apologized over and over for her daughter's behavior. While it was somewhat galling to be overlooked, Kenneth understood Priscilla's excitement upon seeing her grandfather.

As a duke and a bachelor, he was no stranger to dealing with ambitious mamas of unmarried daughters. Margaret Graham took fawning to a new level. Ten minutes spent in a carriage with her was enough. He didn't know if he had the stomach for a lifetime of her as his mother-in-law. She made her dislike of Jock Graham painfully obvious. He'd only just met the fellow, but Jock seemed like the kind of chap anyone could get along with.

After assuring himself a footman had escorted his passenger into the house, he instructed the driver to carry on to the Dower House. He intended to fetch his mother in the expectation she would enjoy meeting Priscilla's grandfather.

He was surprised to find his uncle in the withdrawing room and got the feeling he'd interrupted an important conversation. This lack of deference could become tiresome. He glared at Gregor when he realized his mother had been crying.

"It's all right, Kenneth," she said. "We've been burying the hatchet."

He definitely didn't want to delve into events that had taken place long ago, so he stuck to the plan. "Miss Graham's grandfather has arrived unexpectedly. He's from Galloway and wanted to sample the famous *Uachdaran*, so he came with my cousins..."

His uncle rose from the sofa with a speed that belied his age. "Why did ye nay say so?" he asked.

Kenneth was beginning to wonder if the Scots simply didn't understand the polite deference that was a titled person's due. "I did say so," he muttered. "My barouche awaits."

"Come, Maureen," Gregor cooed, offering his hand. "Let's meet this Lowlander."

"Aye," she replied with a smile.

Kenneth was left alone to ponder this new aspect of his mother's persona. He hadn't seen her so animated for many a year. His own life had tended to become predictable. Being a duke came with onerous responsibilities, but a little fun now and again wouldn't hurt. He'd enjoyed the dance rehearsal. Perhaps it was time to discover if there was a Scot buried deep inside himself.

TAVISH SEEKS A WEALTHY BRIDE

∽

Tavish was fiercely proud of the whisky he and his brothers produced. Thanks to the improvements they'd made through years of experimentation—some successful, some not—it bore little resemblance to the whisky their ancestors had first distilled. He knew in his heart it was a superior single malt.

He'd known instinctively that Jock Graham would be impressed. The man already knew of the brand. However, the hearty endorsement of a fellow Scot meant a lot.

Piper's grandfather was a jovial fellow. Tavish took a liking to him right off. Gregor pulled his leg about being a Lowlander and thus not a true Scot, but the good-natured tit-for-tat ribbing made it plain the two men might become friends.

Jock and Aunty Maureen got along famously from the moment Jock shared his opinion she was far too young and attractive to be the dowager duchess.

The happy gathering put Tavish in mind of a *Ceilidh* back home and *Uachdaran* provided the perfect accompaniment to the relaxed ambience. Piper agreed to sip a wee dram. Tavish wasn't offended by the endearing way she wrinkled her nose. He was pleased to see the roses bloom in her cheeks.

The only person who seemed ill at ease was Lady Graham. She steadfastly refused Aunty Maureen's entreaties to try a wee drop of *Uachdaran*.

Jock ignored her and kept on using his granddaughter's nickname, which didn't surprise Tavish. He'd gleaned from bits and pieces of the conversation in the carriage that mother and grandfather didn't get along. However, Kenneth also gave his future mother-in-law the cold shoulder although he too seemed irritated by the use of the nickname. He steadfastly called his fiancée Priscilla, which she clearly found annoying. It all begged the question—what had gone on during the short ride in the Ramsay barouche and just where did Piper's affections lie?

∽

Piper was enjoying the afternoon immensely. Seated next to her on the settee, her grandfather put an arm around her shoulders and leaned close to her ear. She inhaled the comforting aromas of wool and pipe smoke.

"Seems like a good catch," he whispered.

Contentment fled. Her throat tightened. He was obviously looking at Kenneth, but must have noticed something was amiss. "He disapproves of my nickname," she replied.

"Is that the reason ye dinna wish to marry him?"

"Is it that obvious?" she replied, meshing her nervous fingers together in her lap.

"Yer mother seems intent on your marrying a titled gentleman."

"But I don't love Ramsay," she admitted.

"And ye think love's important?"

Piper took a deep breath, hoping he'd understand what was in her heart. "You should ask my father's opinion on that subject."

He withdrew his arm and clamped both hands on his knees. "Aye, Piper, and there ye have the crux o' the matter. I warned my son about marrying a lass who didna love him, but he was adamant love would grow between them."

"Mother knows, doesn't she?"

"Aye. Ye ken I'm a direct person. Too direct, maybe. I told her I thought the marriage was a mistake."

"And she's never forgiven you."

"Aye. That's doesna mean I was right. They've gotten along well and made a go of it, I suppose. And they gave birth to a wonderful daughter they love very much. But, I drove them away and hardly ever see my darlin' grandlass."

"I think Mama would eventually have insisted on moving to the city where she was born," she said, glad to finally learn the reason for her mother's dislike. "They do respect each other. Most of the time, anyway. But I want more than that from a husband."

"Ye want a passionate *mon,* somebody like, oh let's say, yon Tavish King.*"

"I haven't hidden my feelings very well, have I?"

"Nay, but then neither has he."

"You think he cares for me?"

"The lad's smitten," he chuckled.

Did Piper dare to hope? "But there's the duke to consider."

He patted her hand. "Let me see what I can do."

~

Weeks ago, Maureen had arranged for Priscilla Graham and her son to meet. She had thought the girl would be a good match for Kenneth, but it was becoming increasingly evident that there was no alchemy between them.

On the other hand, Priscilla and Tavish King couldn't look at each other or exchange conversation without sparks flying. She wondered if Gregor had noticed.

"Thirty years ago," she told him, "I gave up everything to elope with Freddie Hawkins."

"Weel," he replied, "nay exactly everything. Ye kent Freddie was wealthy."

"Trust you to see things that way," she said, feigning a hearty punch to his arm.

"And who could ha'e predicted he'd inherit a dukedom?" her brother added.

"True, but I'll forget what I wanted to say if you persist in diverting me."

"*Uachdaran'll* do that," he quipped.

"Be serious. I'm worried about Kenneth. I don't think the Graham girl is the bride for him."

"She seems more taken wi' Tavish."

"And he with her, if I'm not mistaken."

"Aye," he sighed. "I'll speak to him."

"And say what? We both know love doesn't listen to rational arguments."

RECEIVING LINE

On the evening of the ball, Tavish's nervousness grew as the seemingly endless line of carriages drew up in the driveway of Ramsay House. His brothers' uncharacteristic silence confirmed his suspicion they too were apprehensive. Having satisfied Gregor's inspection of their highland finery, they left the chamber to take their places in the receiving line.

Aunty Maureen had insisted they practice earlier in the day, for which Tavish was grateful as the guests began to arrive at the top of the winding staircase. Protocol demanded Kenneth be first in line. As each guest was announced, he greeted them, then introduced his mother and sister. In turn, Aunty Maureen introduced her nephews and brother as the guests of honor.

Tavish was pleasantly surprised and relieved by the warmth of the greetings they received. People admired their Highland garb and asked questions about where they were from. He wasn't shocked no one had heard of Glengeárr.

"It seems most think Edinburgh and Glasgow are the only places o' interest in Scotland," Gregor muttered.

Aunty Maureen's mention of the Kings' famous whisky caused many a raised eyebrow among the gentlemen.

Kenneth had indicated he planned to invite a select few to sample the whisky in the privacy of the library, but Tavish had no way of knowing which guests would be chosen.

"And of course, Sir Oliver, Sir Jock, Lady Margaret and Lady Priscilla Graham need no introduction," Aunty Maureen said, dragging Tavish's attention away from the foppish guest who'd asked him what Scotsmen wore under a kilt. Preoccupied with thinking Uncle Gregor might just answer the giggled question in his own inimitable way, he hadn't noticed the Grahams' arrival.

"Sir Oliver, Sir Jock," he said, offering each a handshake.

"I should have thought to wear my kilt instead of this monkey suit," Sir Jock replied, earning a scowl from his daughter-in-law.

"Aye," Tavish replied, brushing a kiss on the cold hand Lady Margaret proffered.

Then he turned to the stunningly beautiful woman he couldn't stop thinking about. "Piper," he breathed, hoping she understood the longing in his voice and the love in his eyes.

"Tavish," Piper replied. That simple exchange was all it took to confirm they shared a magical connection. The warmth of his lips penetrated her gloves when he brushed a courtly kiss on her knuckles. The heat in his eyes when their gazes met threatened to buckle her knees. For a blessed moment, Piper could ignore her mother's sputtering about scarcely saying a word to the duke. She and Tavish were all that mattered.

"All set for the reel?" he asked with a wink.

"Can't wait," she replied, excited to see he'd also been affected by the recognition of their mutual attraction.

In the blink of an eye, her world had changed. Tavish King was the man she'd been waiting for.

"I understand ye might need another gentleman," her grandfather said. "The butler apparently rounded out numbers at the rehearsal, but he canna join in now."

"Aye," Tavish replied, "are ye volunteering?"

"Try and stop me."

The affectionate exchange between two men who meant so much to her gladdened Piper's heart.

To everyone's surprise, her father chimed in. "You beat me to it, Da," he said.

Nose in the air and jaw clenched, her mother stalked off into the ballroom.

∼

Kenneth was conflicted. He enjoyed his privileged position at the head of the receiving line. Guests greeted him with the respect due his title. Most of the glad-handing and curtseying was genuine, but he was acutely aware that some of the sycophants wouldn't have deigned to speak to him on the street had his father not inherited the dukedom.

Everyone in attendance knew the story and doubtless many snide remarks would be made regarding the Hawkins family's suitability. It angered him that such petty jealous had the potential to hurt his mother. As Duchess of Ramsay, she'd done a great deal to raise the family's standing in society.

In that respect, he was confident his Scottish relatives wouldn't be among the snipers. From the outset, the King brothers had treated him as a long-lost cousin. They could clearly care less about his title.

The snobs would, however, be affronted if they weren't invited to the private whisky tasting later in the evening. Yes, the hypocrites would drink the liquor, eat his food and dance to the music played by musicians he'd hired. But they'd be hard pressed to say anything negative about the quality of *Uachdaran*.

He'd wager even the Regent would hear about the whisky, and the reel. A stellar evening lay ahead.

The only fly in the ointment was the obvious attraction between Tavish and Priscilla. Kenneth's dislike of Lady Graham had only intensified with her fawning, whereas Priscilla had barely said a word to him, all her attention on Tavish.

It was perplexing.

DAISY WAS PLEASED to see Kenneth greet Lady Jasmine Foxworthy. Her mother hadn't understood why she'd wanted the girl and her parents added to the guest list. They weren't friends by any stretch of the imagination. In fact, Daisy couldn't stand Jasmine and the feeling was mutual.

However, she had a plan.

"Lady Jasmine," she cooed, stepping in front of her mother. "How wonderful to see you and your parents. May I introduce my Scottish cousins, Tavish, Payton and Niven King."

The necessary greetings were exchanged. As Daisy hoped, Jasmine quickly gave all her attention to the most handsome King brother, and Payton in turn couldn't take his eyes off Jasmine's scandalous décolletage.

"We're planning a rather exciting Scottish dance demonstration later," Daisy gushed. "But, sadly, Payton has no partner."

"I'll gladly be your partner," Jasmine declared, fluttering her eyelashes.

"Excellent," Payton replied, making no mention of the fact his aunty was his partner. "I'll maybe teach ye a few o' the steps beforehand."

"I'd be delighted," Jasmine sighed.

Feeling immensely satisfied, Daisy watched the Foxworthy trio walk away. Payton and Jasmine were two of a kind. Gold-diggers. He'd be disappointed when he discovered the Foxworthy family's finances were in dire straits.

Maureen had hosted more balls than she could recall. Of course, as the Duchess of Ramsay, she'd stood beside her late husband at the head of the receiving line. Being in the middle of the line was a completely different, and arguably less stressful experience.

She was immensely proud of Kenneth. He was much more comfortable with the role of duke than his father had been, but Freddie had never expected to inherit the title.

She became convinced that Priscilla Graham was more interested in Tavish King than in Kenneth. Her son must have found her behavior hurtful, but he showed no sign of it. Sometimes, she wished he would show more emotion. Keeping things bottled up inside fed a person's anger. It had taken her years to come to terms with Gregor's rejection. Ironically, Freddie's elevation to the peerage had forced her out of the doldrums.

Gregor's presence in the line was a boon that signaled an end to thirty years of rancor. It felt good to have her cantankerous brother by her side, and the borrowed plaid draped across her evening gown drew many a positive comment. She took enormous satisfaction knowing the *ton* never had any idea she was from Scotland until now.

She wondered what Daisy was up to. Apparently, the plan was to throw Payton King and Jasmine Foxworthy together. Daisy didn't like Jasmine, so something had happened to turn her against Payton. And that fickle young man had quickly forgotten he was his aunty's partner. Amazing the effect a generous bosom could have. However, Maureen didn't foresee a long term relationship between Payton and Jasmine. Tavish and the Graham girl—that was a whole different thing.

THE REEL

After light refreshments served in the intermission, Maureen announced that a demonstration reel would be performed in honor of the guests from Scotland. The reaction was perhaps predictably muted.

However, once the reel began and Niven worked his magic with the fiddle, people gradually began clapping and tapping their feet.

Gregor was annoyed that Payton had quickly ditched Maureen as his partner for the reel. All it took was a lass with big tits. His nephew didn't seem to notice the giggling hussy had two left feet.

However, Jock Graham came to Maureen's rescue. It gladdened Gregor's heart to see his sister dance with abandon. She seemed overly free and easy with the Lowlander, but he had sat in judgment before and didn't intend to do it again. God had returned his sister to him and he'd learned his lesson.

Tavish had recovered his confidence and led the

couples through the sequences as only a true Highlander could. Daisy's feet were no doubt relieved. She too seemed happier than he'd seen her since the night of the first dinner at the Dower House.

Gregor got the feeling something had happened to ease Tavish's tension. The Graham girl was happier too. She partnered Kenneth. Poor sod likely didn't even realize she had eyes only for Tavish. He foresaw trouble there.

When a few adventurous souls started eightsomes of their own, Gregor stepped in to call the sequences.

All in all, it augured well for the private tasting event Kenneth had planned.

∼

It no longer mattered to Piper that Tavish wasn't her partner. In a way, he was. A silent message had passed between them. Just knowing Tavish had feelings for her heightened her body's communion with the rhythm of the dance. His kilt swished and whirled as he danced like only a proud Highlander could. He was clearly enjoying himself. He was so very handsome when he smiled.

She even found Kenneth's company enjoyable, though she avoided looking directly at him lest he see more than she wanted him to see. He had to eventually accept she didn't want to marry him, but it was essential his anger not be directed at Tavish.

She was glad people started to clap and tap their feet. Their reaction brought a smile to Kenneth's face. He must have been apprehensive as to how the demonstration would be received. Deviating from the norm wasn't always well accepted by the *ton*. It augured well for the whisky tasting he'd planned for later.

She caught a brief glimpse of her mother's scowling face. Margaret Graham was probably upset because her husband had joined one of the impromptu squares.

It was a joy to see her grandfather dance with the Dowager. They were both grinning like adolescents.

She didn't recognize Payton's partner.

~

Tavish danced like a man reborn. He'd never enjoyed a reel more nor been prouder to be a Scot. His bones absorbed Niven's music. Piper Graham shared the same intense cravings he felt. It made life more complicated, yet it didn't. Angering Kenneth would be the inevitable consequence. His cousin might retaliate by using his influence to sabotage the plans for *Uachdaran*. So be it. Tavish had no intention of not pursuing Piper.

His Aunty Maureen was getting along well with Piper's grandfather. One would think they'd danced together for years. He hoped she would understand his actions regarding Piper.

Gregor wouldn't.

His uncle would simply have to accept they'd have to find other ways to finance the improvements they wanted to make. Payton and Niven would come around.

He chuckled inwardly. Piper had mentioned money from her grandfather. He didn't care if she came with a dowry or not. He wanted her. She was the woman for him.

It came to him that his cousin Daisy was enjoying the reel more than she had at the rehearsal. Probably because he wasn't stomping on her toes! She didn't seem upset that Payton was salivating over his new partner. She must have lost interest in him. Good thing. Wedding a cousin was never a good idea. Many a highland clan had proven that over the centuries.

∽

Maureen hadn't had so much fun in years. Duchesses didn't let their hair down and dance Scottish reels with handsome rogues they'd just met. She'd loved her husband and gladly supported him in his new role as Duke of Ramsay. It had been a labor of love. But Freddie was gone and Maureen intended to make up for lost time. Kenneth was the duke now. She would support him. However, she thirsted to rediscover the Maureen she'd left behind.

Kenneth would need her sympathy when he realized Priscilla was in love with Tavish. She hoped he was man enough to take the rejection for what it was—Dame Fortune smiling down on him. The right woman would come along. The Graham girl wasn't that woman.

∽

"I was surprised to be invited," Jasmine confided to Payton as they circled clockwise.

Pleased she was finally getting the hang of the steps, he'd had time to ponder why Daisy had finagled the two of them to be partners. He'd readily fallen into the trap she set. When would he learn not to focus all his attention on a lass' breasts? Jasmine's were on full display and he had to admit they were extraordinarily tempting. At least his Aunty Maureen didn't look upset that he'd abandoned her as a partner. Jock Graham was her age anyway and, from the look of it, she was probably having more fun dancing with him.

"Daisy and I don't get along," Jasmine added as the circle moved counterclockwise.

Now, he understood. For some reason, his cousin was angry with him. She apparently thought matching him with Jasmine would end badly. "Well, Miss Foxworthy," he crooned, inhaling her enticing perfume as he swung her into the teapot sequence, "I'm verra glad ye were invited, and that ye're my partner."

THE TASTING

Kenneth had planned the private whisky tasting with great care. He and Mainwaring had compiled a list of male guests based on strict criteria. Yet, Gregor seemed intent on questioning his choices even as the moment to begin drew near. "They are men known for their discernment when it comes to spirits," he told his uncle for the umpteenth time.

"Aye, so ye said, but..."

"They are not prone to drunkenness, if that's what you're afraid of."

"Nay, but..."

"They are titled men of influence at court and in the investment community."

"But ye only invited a handful."

"This is my world, Uncle. You must trust my judgment. And I ask that you let me do the talking."

His uncle nodded, but the stern set of his jaw belied his willingness to cooperate.

The privileged few were already making their

discreet way to the library. Tavish, Payton and Niven were on the move as well. Kenneth was sorely tempted to exclude Gregor, but then the old man would put up a fuss. Espying Jock Graham in the crowd, he had an idea. "Uncle, can I ask you to pass on an invitation for Priscilla's grandfather to accompany you?"

Thunder darkened his uncle's face. "A Lowlander?"

Kenneth counted to ten, a habit that seemed to be more and more necessary these days. "He'll be an asset. He already loves *Uachdaran*."

"I suppose ye're right."

A few minutes later, Kenneth breathed again when Jock smiled broadly and shook the scowling Gregor's hand.

He set off for the library, confident things would go well—if he managed to untie the knot in his gut and pretend he hadn't noticed Tavish's attempts to steal Priscilla's affections.

∼

OLIVER GRAHAM WAS SMUGLY pleased to find himself among a select group of titled gentlemen in the Duke of Ramsay's library. It didn't matter that Kenneth Hawkins had only invited him because he was Piper's...er...Priscilla's father.

And therein lay his dilemma. Margaret was pushing hard for their daughter to marry the duke when it was quite obvious she favored the King lad. He couldn't in all good conscience consign Piper to a loveless marriage. He'd ignored his father's warnings and ended up with a wife who'd turned into a shrew. He didn't blame Margaret. It must be hard for a woman to be married to a man she didn't love. He'd done all he could to win her favor—even left his beloved Scotland. But if there was no love...

He'd have to have a word with Kenneth Hawkins. Thwarting a duke was a daunting prospect. Feeling like a useless coward, he was about to slip away when his father entered with the elderly Scottish fellow. It was hard to believe Gregor was the Dowager Duchess' brother.

~

Tavish didn't have time to inform his brothers of his decision. He had to hope they'd understand. His honor wouldn't allow him to participate in Kenneth's tasting event without clearing the air between them.

His cousin's frosty glare was proof enough he'd noticed the chemistry between himself and Piper. He took advantage of the guests' excited chatter to take Kenneth aside. "I'll understand if ye dinna have yer heart in this evening's tasting," he said. "But I want to make it clear I intend to pursue a relationship with Piper Graham."

Kenneth narrowed his eyes. "You're direct, I'll grant you that."

"I'm a Scot," he replied.

"Aye," Kenneth quipped. "I can't say I'm happy about your trespassing, but this event is purely business. I sense there's money to be made with *Uachdaran*, so personal feelings can't enter into it."

Tavish should have felt relief, but he didn't. For him, distilling whisky wasn't just a business. It was his life's calling, his passion. Whisky had been the love of his life until Piper came along. "I suppose it's too much to hope you and I can still be friends."

"This isn't the time or place, Cousin. Our guests are getting restless. I'd appreciate your help with any questions about the distilling process, and try to keep our uncle under control."

Kenneth strode away to greet his friends. The evening would be a success. His cousin would make sure of it. If the only negative thing was a cruel remark about Gregor, then so be it. Kenneth was perhaps entitled.

Tavish was satisfied he'd made the right decision by being honest and up front. There would likely be further repercussions he couldn't yet predict, but Piper was worth it.

∽

NIVEN HAPPILY SOAKED up the effusive compliments about his fiddle playing. He'd been nervous about interacting with this select group of Kenneth's high society friends, but they seemed pleasant enough fellows. It wasn't the first time music had helped ease his way. He'd never had Tavish's confidence, nor Payton's larger-than-life personality.

He was musing on this truth when Kenneth's voice

penetrated. "Niven, would you explain the hand turning of the malt to our guests?"

He glanced at Tavish who'd always been the acknowledged spokesperson. His older brother nodded his assent, so he embarked on an explanation he could probably recite in his sleep. Eyes wide, the guests continued to sip the whisky, apparently impressed by what he'd said.

"Perhaps Payton can elaborate on the importance of burning peat in the kilns," Kenneth suggested a few minutes later. "*Uachdaran* is unique in that regard."

Payton obliged, but he too sported a puzzled frown. Their ducal cousin was clearly ignoring Tavish who, astonishingly, didn't seem upset.

~

THE TASTING event wasn't proceeding the way Gregor thought it would go. By rights, he and Tavish should be doing all the talking. What did Kenneth know about distilling whisky?

However, perhaps his nephew was right. This wasn't Gregor's world and the toffs were clearly impressed by the whisky and the story behind its development.

The smiles stayed on the nodding guests' faces even when Kenneth embarked on the notion of investment.

Gregor cleared his throat, intending to explain the idea of special barrels, but the cursed Lowlander spoke before he had the chance.

"And what will our funds be used for?" Jock Graham asked.

Gregor had to grudgingly admit it was a clever question that assumed the group's investment was a foregone conclusion and opened the door for Tavish to at last speak. His nephew's explanation of aging whisky in sherry barrels resulted in exclamations of delighted surprise.

Had Gregor been in charge, he'd have asked for a commitment right then and there. He realized that would have been a mistake when Kenneth brought the event to a close by saying, "My man of business will be in touch, gentlemen. I'm sure many of you know Richard Mainwaring."

Standing discreetly to one side, Mainwaring bowed.

The conversation was animated as the guests filed out of the library, raising Gregor's hopes that the lads might not be obliged to marry after all.

WAR CRY

No one remarked on the absence from the ballroom of a dozen dukes, earls and viscounts. The men who hadn't been invited to the private tasting took the opportunity to dance with different partners. Piper should have been elated to be danced off her feet but, with Tavish gone, it was as though there was no air to breathe.

Her mind filled with plotting ways to speak privately with the man she couldn't stop thinking about. If he was as smitten with her as she was with him, they'd have to tell Kenneth.

That might mean the end of the duke's interest in helping the Kings raise money for the distillery. She would have her grandfather's inheritance when she came of age, but perhaps she wasn't being practical. Was her desire for passion and romance stealing away her common sense? After all, Tavish lived in a remote part of Scotland.

All her doubts flew away like chaff on the wind when

she espied Tavish reenter the ballroom deep in conversation with her grandfather. She faltered when she realized the two men looked annoyed.

~

Jock Graham had mixed emotions about Tavish confiding his feelings for Piper. Surprise wasn't one of them. It was clear to anyone with eyes that Tavish and Piper were meant for each other.

Personally, he was delighted by the prospect of his granddaughter wedding a Scot, even if Tavish was a Highlander. He liked the King boy and admired his work ethic. He doubted the *Uachdaran* distillery would have flourished as it had without Tavish's firm hand at the helm. The other brothers might reel off an account of the process and share in the hard work, but he suspected it was Tavish who'd proposed they hand turn the malt regularly and use peat in the kilns. And Tavish wouldn't just send his workers out to dig peat. He'd be up to his armpits in the wretched stuff. The notion of aging whisky in sherry barrels was obviously Tavish's brainchild, and Kenneth had finally given him the opportunity to explain.

The duke's deliberate snubbing of the elder King spoke volumes. He'd definitely noticed Piper's ogling of the Scot. Therein lay a dilemma. Angering a duke was dangerous, but it had to be done, for Piper's sake. The more daunting prospect was further alienating his daughter-in-law. Margaret would fight tooth and nail to make her daughter a duchess. Her failure to accomplish that goal would drive another wedge between Jock and his son.

"Go back to the library," he told Tavish. "I'll fetch Piper."

∼

Tavish was relieved the library was empty save for a couple of servants tidying up the last of the glasses.

He paced the room, wondering why it was so infernally hot when there was no fire in the cold grate. Scant minutes ago, in this very library, he'd taken part in an event that had the potential to open up a whole new world for him and his brothers. Yet, he was more nervous now as he waited for Piper and her grandfather.

He'd never risked his heart before. He'd be gutted if she didn't feel the same intense cravings. Was he fooling himself? A city girl like Piper wouldn't want to live in the Highlands.

He stopped breathing when the door opened.

Then Piper was in his arms, raining kisses on his face.

His heart and his manhood soared as he gathered her to his body and pressed his lips to hers. The ancient war cry of the MacGregors echoed in his head. *"Ard Choille."* He'd come home to the *high wood*.

A polite cough broke them apart.

Breathing hard, he looked into Piper's eyes and saw the love he'd craved all his adult life, but feared he'd never find. "Lass," he growled. "Will ye be mine?"

"I am yours, Tavish," she replied. "Forever."

"A hard life in the Highlands is all I have to offer ye," he admitted.

"A life without you would be no life at all."

Her grandfather cleared his throat again. "Ye'd best both be sure o' this. There'll be repercussions."

"I'm sure," Tavish replied.

"As am I," Piper assured him.

∼

ANXIOUS NOT TO GIVE AWAY HER presence outside the library, Maureen held her breath and leaned back against the paneled wall. Her foolishly adolescent reason for being there—to follow Jock Graham—had caused a pulse to thunder in her throat. After overhearing Tavish and Priscilla's declarations of love, she felt like her heart was about to burst from her chest. Grief for Kenneth surged. "My boy," she murmured, afraid her son was about to get his heart broken.

She clenched her fists, admitting inwardly she also harbored selfish fears. A rift with the Graham family would mean never seeing Jock again. It was lunacy—a woman her age, a widow. But she'd found joy in the short time spent with the Lowlander. She'd laughed again, felt she had a reason to live. Perhaps she'd simply imbibed too much whisky in the last wee while. Swallowing hard, she summoned the courage that had seen her through many difficulties over the years and flounced away from the library, chin in the air. She'd survived great losses before and would do so again. She was a Scot, after all.

A WORD, IF YOU PLEASE

J ock advised Tavish and Piper to return separately to the ballroom. For a while, he feared he might have to pry them apart, but eventually they saw the wisdom of taking things one step at a time. Jock's first step was to seek out his son.

When he entered the ballroom and met Margaret's hostile glare, it occurred to him Oliver wasn't the person he'd have to convince. "Might I have a word?" he asked after brushing a courtly kiss on his daughter-in-law's knuckles.

The out of character gesture may have been a mistake. She snatched her hand away and stiffened her shoulders. "I'm not interested in anything you have to say," she declared.

"Weel, Margaret," he replied. "Ye can cling to yer resentment o'me and destroy yer wee lass in the process, or ye can swallow yer pride and listen."

She pursed her lips but didn't walk away.

"I dinna fault ye fer wanting Piper to become a

duchess, and she'd make a fine duchess—if she loved the duke ye are pushing her to marry."

"And just what would you know about it?" she hissed.

"I ken Piper doesna love Kenneth. She's in love wi' someone else. But ye likely ken more about loveless marriages than I do."

Her eyes welled with tears. He regretted inflicting pain but his arrow had hit home. "She's going to seek yer blessing. I hope ye'll grant it. Talk it o'er wi' Oliver. Ye both want what's best."

～

GREGOR WAS FUMING by the time he tracked down his nephew. Tavish immediately recognized his mood. "What's amiss, Uncle?" he asked.

"A word, if ye please," he growled. "I just spoke wi' my sister. She wouldna reveal why she was upset. *Ask Jock and Tavish*, she said. If that Lowlander did something to upset her..."

"Nay," Tavish replied. "She must have o'erheard us talking in the library."

"Us?"

"I plan to marry Piper Graham."

Gregor stared, certain he must have misheard. "Ye canna wed the lass. She's promised to yer cousin. Besides, if Kenneth's friends invest in the distillery, ye lads willna need to wed."

"I'm sorry," Tavish replied. "I ken ye willna understand, but Piper is the woman I've searched for all my life."

"But Kenneth will scupper the deal if ye steal his lass."

"She's nay his lass. She doesna love him and never agreed to marry him. If he retaliates, so be it."

Gregor feared his head might explode. "*So be it*, ye say, ye cocky mongrel. Ye'll risk everything fer a bit o' skirt?"

"I'll pretend I didna hear that," Tavish growled before striding away.

∽

KENNETH HAD NEVER SEEN A VOLCANO, but he'd heard the tale of the total destruction of Pompeii. It was common knowledge that Vesuvius gave the people of the Roman city plenty of warning of the disaster to come. The problem was they'd never seen a volcanic eruption and didn't understand the significance of the earth tremors and the pumice raining down on their city for days.

He felt rather like those ancient folk. Something cataclysmic was happening. Tavish had tried to warn him but he'd dismissed the possibility Priscilla would refuse his proposal.

Even in his pleasant whisky-induced haze, he realized he hadn't actually got round to proposing.

Talk about head in the sand! He'd assumed Miss Graham understood his intentions. She may have but she'd made her lack of interest quite obvious. He'd been too wrapped up in his own ducal importance and eminent suitability as a spouse. Meanwhile, she'd fallen for his cousin, a Scot who wore a kilt and distilled whisky.

It was humbling.

He wanted to weep like a babe deprived of its favorite plaything, but dukes didn't indulge in such maudlin behavior. They shrugged off the disappointment, or they got even.

In the meanwhile, he was still the host of a ball that, so far, had been a success. The musicians played on and the dance floor was full. His Scottish relatives were chatting with some of the men who'd attended the tasting. Gregor was the only one scowling, but that wasn't unusual. A few people had left, given the lateness of the hour, but many familiar faces lingered. Among them the Grahams—and Oliver was headed his way, his face scrunched in a fierce grimace. His spirits flagged. It was more than obvious what the curious fellow had plucked up the courage to say, but did he have to look as though the executioner awaited? Informing a duke his proposal of marriage wasn't acceptable must be daunting.

"Might I have a word?" Oliver rasped.

Kenneth had a decision to make, but he made it quickly. Oliver Graham was a nice enough chap—henpecked, but... "I'll save you the trouble, Oliver," he replied. "I've withdrawn my suit for your daughter's hand."

For an alarming moment, he feared the man might swoon with relief, but the color returned to his pudgy face and he babbled his way out of Kenneth's presence.

"That felt surprisingly good," he muttered under his

breath. It struck him that perhaps Priscilla wasn't the right choice. She was physically beautiful and endearingly charming, but his cock had never managed to rouse itself in her presence. A cold chill crept up his spine. Perhaps there was something amiss with his equipment.

∽

"You'd better speak to the duke," Piper's mother said.

Piper had seen her father approach Kenneth and wondered what they'd discussed. Neither seemed happy. She also wasn't sure what her mother was implying. Did her parents know what had transpired between her and Tavish? Whatever the case, she was obliged to tell Kenneth directly that she couldn't marry him. If she'd had the courage to be honest before matters had gone this far...but disappointing her parents had weighed heavily on her mind. "I will speak to him," she replied. "But you may not like what I have to tell him."

Tears welled when her mother kissed her on each cheek and said, "I trust you to do the right thing."

Uncertain what to make of the ambiguous statement, Piper approached Kenneth who was closeted in an alcove, deep in conversation with the Dowager Duchess. Plucking up her courage, she asked, "Might I have a word, Your Grace?"

"Certainly, Piper," he replied as he got to his feet.

The Dowager's eyes widened as she rose to leave. She too had taken note of her son's use of her nickname.

Piper sat in the chair Her Grace had vacated, taking courage from the warmth of the velvet. "I have no wish to offend, but I should have made it clear before now that I cannot marry you, Ramsay."

Her heart raced when he took hold of her hand. "I am not offended, though I should point out I never actually proposed marriage."

Heat flooded her face. "Er...I assumed..."

He meshed his fingers with hers. "Don't worry. Had I not been so certain no woman would ever reject me as a spouse, I would have realized you and I aren't suited."

Piper's stiff shoulders relaxed. "I hope we can remain friends," she tried.

She was escaping unscathed, but did he know about her commitment to Tavish?

"Of course. And I still intend to promote my cousins' whisky venture," he assured her.

~

MAUREEN PASTED a smile on her face as she circulated among the remaining guests, many of whom were preparing to leave Ramsay House. They couldn't know the turmoil roiling in her heart. Kenneth had accepted the news of Tavish as his rival with good grace. He seemed resigned to not marrying the Graham girl. He'd always had a tendency to keep his emotions under tight control. She'd reassured him the right woman would eventually come along, but a broken heart doesn't often listen to trite words of comfort. She could only hope for the best for her son, but at least now she could continue to enjoy Jock Graham's company.

Selfish guilt pecked at her.

REPERCUSSIONS

Tavish intended to bid Piper farewell with a wee kiss of reassurance, but Gregor bustled his nephews into his chamber before he had the chance.

"Yer brother has put all yer futures at risk," his uncle declared.

Tavish clenched his jaw in the face of his brothers' puzzled frowns. "Let me explain," he growled.

Gregor pointed an accusing finger. "Stole yer cousin's fiancée," he hissed.

"Ye and Piper Graham?" Payton asked.

"Aye," Tavish confessed. "But I didna steal her. Kenneth never asked her to marry him."

"Any fool can see ye and Piper belong together," Niven said. "If it means losing our ducal cousin's support, so be it."

"Aye," Payton agreed, clamping a hand on Tavish's shoulder. "She's the perfect lass for ye."

Gregor sulked. "Ye mean to say…"

"Do ye nay understand?" Niven asked their uncle. "Our brother's happiness is more important than anything else. He's always considered our welfare before his own. I'm glad he's found someone who loves him."

Payton nodded. "Think on the marvels Tavish accomplished when he wasna happily married. Piper will be an asset to the business."

Humbled, Tavish swallowed the lump in his throat and embraced his brothers.

"Aye, now I think on it, the Graham lass did say she had money to invest," Gregor muttered.

Tavish and his brothers chuckled at their uncle's predictable reasoning.

∼

The Graham family's ride home was uncomfortable. The carriage wasn't designed for four adults, particularly when two of them were broad-shouldered, long-legged men like Piper's father and grandfather.

However, it wasn't the cramped circumstances that made the atmosphere awkward.

Piper believed most mothers and daughters shared the excitement of an impending marriage, but Lady Margaret Graham wedged herself in a corner and refused to participate in a conversation.

Her husband tried several times to engage her, but she snatched her hand away and continued to sulk.

Piper resolved then and there that if she ever bore a daughter, she would not force the child to be something she wasn't.

She smiled at her father in an effort to let him know she didn't blame him, but it was probably too dark for him to see. It had never been more painfully obvious that Oliver Graham's love for his wife wasn't reciprocated.

Grandad Jock's presence was the light in the darkness. He held Piper's hand and, without uttering a word, let her know everything would be all right.

∽

"I'm glad you decided to stay over at the main house with us, Mama," Daisy said after the last guests had left.

"As am I," her mother replied with a yawn. "I'm too tired to think about returning to the Dower House this late at night."

"I think it went well," Daisy said softly.

"Indeed," her mother agreed.

Seated in his favorite armchair in the library, Kenneth drew on his cigar, blew a very satisfying smoke ring and sipped his glass of *Uachdaran*. The ball hadn't turned out precisely how he'd expected, but he was strangely in agreement with the two most important women in his life. However, much as he loved them, he wasn't willing to divulge everything that had happened just yet.

Kenneth blew another smoke ring, pondering the tendency of people to indulge in small talk when life-changing events had taken place a short time before. Surprisingly, his sister hadn't refused a glass of whisky when they'd retired to the library. He wasn't ready to talk about his own circumstances, so he decided to bait Daisy. "Explain Jasmine Foxworthy."

His sister shrugged. "What is there to explain?"

"Why was she invited and why did you push her and Payton together?"

"I thought they would suit," she replied.

"Your blush betrays you," he accused.

"Kenneth is right," his mother remarked. "However, I fear your ploy may have misfired. Payton and Jasmine seemed to get along famously."

"That will change when he finds out her family is penniless," she hissed, before taking a gulp of whisky.

Kenneth smirked when she grimaced and almost choked, but he also detected the vitriol in her voice. "What do you mean?"

"He's a gold-digger. The Kings came here to wed wealthy heiresses."

Kenneth couldn't help himself. He stubbed out his cigar, got to his feet and announced, "Well, Tavish has ruined that plan with his choice of Priscilla Graham."

˷

HER ADULT SON would resent being hugged like a child, but Maureen rose quickly and put her arms around him before he could escape. "The right woman will come along, Kenneth."

To her relief, he didn't pull away.

"I know, Mama," he replied, resting his chin on the top of her head. "It's my pride that's hurt more than my heart."

"You're saying Tavish and Priscilla..." Daisy began.

Slowly, Kenneth pulled away from Maureen's embrace. His resigned smile touched her heart. He knew she loved him. He was man enough to weather this storm. "I suppose I've known from the start that Miss Graham wasn't the right one," he confessed.

"Now you mention it," Daisy said. "Tavish and Piper did seem drawn to one another on the day we rehearsed the reel."

"Yes," Maureen agreed. "And we must wish them well. I know only too well what it is to be punished by one's family for falling in love."

"But what will happen with the investment in the distillery?" Daisy asked.

Maureen watched her son struggle with the demon of jealous resentment, relieved for him when his features relaxed.

"I see no reason to abandon the plan," he said. "The Kings are family and we Hawkins have Scottish blood in our veins. What could be more appropriate than investing in a whisky distillery?"

Maureen's heart filled with pride. The heritage she feared lost forever might yet be resurrected.

DEVELOPMENTS

No one was more surprised than Tavish when it was Kenneth who took it upon himself to open a discussion on how the family intended to celebrate the betrothal of his cousin and Miss Graham.

Relief flooded the faces of everyone at the breakfast table and suddenly they were all talking at once. Even Daisy and Payton exchanged a few polite words.

Kenneth undertook to arrange for an announcement in *The Times*. It wasn't important to Tavish but his Aunty Maureen pointed out the *ton's* expectations in that regard.

"'Tis the custom in Scotland for the bride's family to host a reception," Gregor said.

"I fear that won't turn out well if Lady Margaret Graham is involved," Kenneth replied with a wry grin. "She had her heart set on Priscilla marrying a duke."

"To be frank," Tavish interjected. "Most of the people

I care about are here at this table. Why not just invite Piper's parents and grandfather?"

"An intimate supper party," Aunty Maureen declared. "Splendid. I'll host it at the Dower House. Wednesday next, if that suits."

"Grand," Gregor replied.

∽

"I'm truly happy for Tavish," Payton told Niven after everyone had left the breakfast nook. "Back home, I was glad to help thwart the marriage plans of unattached lasses simply because I knew Tavish hadn't met anyone he wished to marry."

"Aye," Niven agreed. "My feelings exactly."

Encouraged by this rare confession from his shy younger brother, Payton took a risk. "I have to tell ye," he began, "I was nervous about Gregor's assertion that love wasna an important consideration in this scheme to wed women with hefty dowries."

"Aye," Niven repeated. "We both ken Tavish shielded us from much of our unhappy parents' anger. None of us wants to endure that kind of loveless marriage."

Payton regretted that he'd never discussed such personal feelings with Niven before. "Ye've grown up when I wasna payin' attention," he admitted.

"Tavish deserves happiness and Piper Graham is just the lass who can provide it."

"I agree, little brother," he teased, ruffling Niven's golden locks. "And I might just have found the right lass for me as well."

"The one with big tits pourin' o'er top of a scandalous frock?" Niven quipped making a lewd gesture with his hands.

"Aye, Jasmine's her name," Payton chuckled in reply. "But let's keep it betwixt me and thee for the moment. Tavish deserves his day in the sun."

∽

The fine weather prompted Maureen to walk back to the Dower House after breakfast.

"I'll come with ye," Gregor said. "I doot there'll be news of investors until the morrow."

"It's almost a mile," Maureen warned.

"Ye think I canna walk a mile?" he asked.

Maureen acknowledged he probably walked everywhere in Glengeárr and was likely fitter than she was. "Very well. Meet me in the foyer in ten minutes."

He proffered his arm as they left the house and walked in companionable silence for a few minutes. Maureen was struck again by the relief she felt being back on good terms with her brother. However, she was certain he would eventually voice his opinion of recent developments. It was too much to expect he'd changed his judgmental ways.

"So," he began. "What's yer opinion o' Tavish and this Graham lass?"

This was an unexpected tack on the part of a man who normally jumped in with both feet. She'd have to navigate carefully. "Aye. You must be happy our nephew has found the right woman."

The stern set of his jaw betrayed his turmoil. When she'd found the right man, he'd banished her from his life.

"I suppose," he replied noncommittally.

Maureen was on her own turf now, no longer the timid lass she'd been thirty years ago. Her older brother had lost the power to intimidate her. "Love has a way of strengthening people, Gregor. The distillery won't suffer if Tavish marries a woman he loves. You came here seeking brides for the lads."

"Aye," he agreed. "I just didna count on things being so complicated."

"That's life," she replied, deeming it too soon to reveal her attraction to Jock Graham.

∼

After breakfast, Kenneth withdrew to his study where Mainwaring waited. He was anxious to learn how things had gone with the potential investors.

"Good news," Richard declared. "Halstead and Lyon sought me out and gave firm commitments. I'll make appointments with their secretaries."

"Well done," Kenneth replied. "Halstead's dukedom at Withenshawe provides him with more money than God, but he's a shrewd investor. The rest will fall into line if he makes good on his promise."

He startled when a knock at the door heralded Tavish. Mainwaring would deem it odd if he didn't share the good news. "I assume you've come for an update.

Two gentlemen have made commitments," he informed his cousin.

Tavish nodded. "Ye did yer utmost to promote our distillery, and I thank ye."

"We're family," he replied, surprised when Tavish shot a hesitant glance at Mainwaring.

"Actually," his cousin said. "I came on a more personal errand."

Mainwaring took his cue and left quietly.

"I want ye to know," Tavish began, "I wouldna have followed up on my feelings for Miss Graham if ye'd been betrothed to her. 'Tisna my nature to trespass."

Kenneth recognized the truth in the statement. Tavish was a proud Scot who prized his honor. However, the loss of Priscilla was still fresh. "You'll answer to me if you harm her in any way," he menaced, sounding too much like an aggrieved parent for his liking.

A puzzled frown creased Tavish's brow. "I love her," he replied. "I willna hurt her."

"I know," Kenneth confessed, offering his hand. "I'm still jealous, but I'll get over it."

To his surprise, Tavish not only accepted the gesture, but pulled him into a hearty embrace. He suspected his cousin didn't often show such emotion.

"Ye're a true gentleman," Tavish said hoarsely. "Ye willna be sorry ye've placed yer trust in me and our distillery. By the by, *Uachdaran* isna simply a business for us."

"Aye," Kenneth replied. "It's your passion."

Tavish shook his hand vigorously. "Maybe ye're a Scot after all," he said with a grin.

They were interrupted by Harrison's loud throat clearing. "A messenger, Your Grace," he intoned.

"Have Mainwaring take the particulars," Kenneth replied, reluctant to end the conversation with his cousin. He had no brothers. Tavish had two and knew what it was to shoulder heavy responsibilities. Sisters simply weren't on the same plane.

Harrison dithered in the doorway. "The messenger from Carlton House is required to wait for your personal reply, Your Grace."

"The message is from the Regent?" Kenneth asked, his gut suddenly feeling the aftereffects of over-imbibing the night before.

∽

Upon returning home from Ramsay House the previous evening, Piper's parents had immediately retired without a word about what had happened at the ball. She'd slept fitfully, dreading the argument that would inevitably dominate the breakfast table.

To her surprise, her father wasn't hiding behind his newspaper. "Good morning, Piper," he declared with a warm smile.

She expected at least a snort from her mother. Nothing was forthcoming, so she took a risk. "Good morning, Mama."

Her parents exchanged a curious glance. She was accustomed to her mother controlling the conversation, but Lady Margaret couldn't meet her husband's gaze. "Good morning, Daughter," she muttered.

"Your mother and I have discussed the events of last night," her father began.

She steeled herself for bad news. They would never sanction a marriage to a man who distilled whisky and lived in the wilds of Scotland.

"We are delighted you've found the right man," he continued. "Aren't we, Margaret, my love?"

Conflicting emotions played out on her mother's face. Piper couldn't see her hands but imagined her fists were clenched beneath the table. Then, a miracle! Lady Margaret's features softened. "I cannot deny I would have preferred you marry a titled English gentleman. However, I agree that your happiness comes first and, if Tavish King makes you happy..."

Piper may have knocked dishes and cutlery to the carpeted floor as she launched herself across the table. She didn't care. "Thank you, Mama," she exclaimed tearfully, though she recognized it was her father she should be thanking.

FIT FOR A WOULD-BE KING

Hands clamped on his knees, Tavish gazed around at the gilded opulence of the anteroom in which he, Kenneth and his brothers sat.

They'd been summoned to Carlton House by the Regent and Kenneth was unusually fidgetty.

The *invitation* had come without explanation, except that the Duke of Ramsay and his Scottish cousins would be expected to attend His Majesty after luncheon.

Tavish knew of the Prince's unpopularity. Scots in particular were offended by his reputation for extravagance and over-indulgence.

It was perhaps as well that Gregor had gone to the Dower House with his sister and knew nothing of the regal audience. He would have insisted on being included and, in some perverse way, Tavish almost wished his no-nonsense uncle was present. His Majesty likely wouldn't know what to make of Gregor's inevitable condemnation of the Regent's Hanoverian uncle and his butchery in the aftermath of Culloden.

The urge to chuckle fled when a nearby set of intricately carved double doors opened and they were ushered into the Regent's presence.

The cartoons Tavish had glimpsed accurately portrayed the prince's florid complexion and bloated features. He looked uncomfortable in an ill-fitting black suit with a tight neckcloth at his throat.

Reluctantly, the King brothers followed Kenneth's lead and bowed. Tavish shouldn't have been surprised to see one of last evening's guests standing beside the Regent's massive chair.

~

As soon as Kenneth saw William Halstead, Duke of Withenshawe, he knew why he'd been summoned. However, that didn't explain the pouting Regent's obvious anger.

"We are displeased, Ramsay," Prince George declared.

Kenneth hadn't seen the Regent since his father's funeral over a year ago, but he'd heard rumors about the weight gain. Bloated jowls and pudgy hands confirmed the gossip. The elaborately tied neckcloth looked like it might choke the life out of the royal. He inhaled, glad that His Majesty had at least come directly to the point. "I apologize if I have offended Your Highness in any way. May I introduce my cousins, the Scottish Kings?"

Realizing his error when a puzzled frown further

creased the Regent's brow, he soldiered on. "Tavish, Payton and Niven King, Your Majesty."

"We bid the Kings welcome to England," Prince George muttered, what might have been a smile thankfully twitching at the corners of his mouth.

Halstead coughed into his fist, apparently hesitant to display amusement, lest the Regent wasn't actually amused by the *double entendre*.

"Our interest in all things Scottish is well known, yet you failed to invite us to an evening of Scottish dancing and whisky tasting."

"A thousand pardons, Majesty," Kenneth replied, wishing his mother were present to hear this regal whining. "I did not think our humble gathering worthy of..."

The Regent waved him to silence. "Withenshawe tells me the whisky is excellent. Did you bring a sample?"

Here was the crux of the matter. The prince didn't care about *all things Scottish*. It was a taste of *Uachdaran* he craved. Kenneth had toyed with the idea of bringing a bottle, but then dismissed is as presumptuous. It really was time he started thinking like a Scot.

∽

Tavish stepped forward, reached into his sporran and pulled out the only memento of his father he'd wanted to keep. "Just a wee dram for ye to taste, Yer Majesty."

Walter King was likely turning over in his grave—his precious embossed pewter flask being handed over to a Hanoverian.

It was a family heirloom of sorts, a souvenir from

France, but if this fat prince was impressed with *Uachdaran*...

A handful of footmen appeared out of nowhere when the Regent snapped his fingers. One snatched the flask from Tavish, unscrewed the top and poured a generous amount into a crystal glass perched on a silver tray held by another footman. This servant then bowed and presented the beverage to his regal master.

It was a mystery how these men had known to be prepared, but Tavish was more interested in watching the prince's reaction as he sipped the whisky.

"By George," the Regent exclaimed, prompting Kenneth's friend to again cough into his fist. "You were right, Withenshawe. Superb. Is there more in the flask?"

∽

Having eaten a splendid lunch and spent a pleasant afternoon chatting about old times with his sister, Gregor walked back to Ramsay House. A stiff breeze had cooled things off, so he walked briskly, humming a lament he was fond of. He increased his speed when he reached the driveway and saw Kenneth and his nephews tumble out of the carriage, all talking at once. "Where have ye been?" he demanded breathlessly.

"Dinna fash, Uncle," Payton replied. "Ye ken the auld rhyme, *Pussy cat, pussy cat, where have ye been? We've been to London to visit the queen?* Weel, we've been to visit the Regent."

"Ye're soused," he exclaimed, brandishing his staff as he followed the laughing quartet into the house.

Kenneth led the way into the withdrawing room where they collapsed onto the settees. "No, Uncle," he said. "We're not drunk, but we've had an exhilarating experience."

Gregor had expected Kenneth would still be licking his wounds after Piper's rejection, but here he was, laughing along with the rest of the giddy fools. "And am I permitted to know what ye've been up to?"

He immediately regretted the words. He truly didn't want to know if his nephews had visited a bawdy house or...

"We were summoned to see the Prince Regent," Tavish said.

"Nay?"

"Aye. And he was unhappy we didn't invite him to our evening of Scottish dancing," Kenneth said. "Wait till I tell my mother! She'll laugh herself silly."

"He claims to be interested in anything to do wi' Scotland," Payton added. "Can ye picture him dancing a reel?"

"What he was really after was a taste o' *Uachdaran*," Tavish declared with a grin.

"And?"

"I gave him Da's flask."

"And?"

"He loves it," Niven exclaimed. "He's thinking o' granting us a royal warrant."

Gregor had to sit down before his legs gave out. "'Tis beyond my wildest dreams."

"Aye," Tavish replied. "But there's a catch."

Piper fidgeted with the fringe of the antimacassar covering the arm of her easy chair. Her parents sat side by side on the adjacent love seat. She couldn't recall ever seeing them hold hands before.

Her grandfather stood behind her chair. She couldn't see him but felt his reassuring presence.

A note had been delivered earlier that morning with the news that Tavish King intended to call on the Grahams this very afternoon.

Her father got to his feet when sounds of his arrival reached them from the foyer. The deafening beat of her erratic heart eased as soon as Tavish was shown into the withdrawing room by Higgins. She loved him. His smile spoke of his love for her. All would be well.

She faltered, shocked when Kenneth followed her beloved. Her mother's wide eyes betrayed her surprise, and perhaps a glint of hope?

"Welcome, gentlemen," her father said, extending his hand to the duke, then to Tavish. "Please be seated."

"We'll remain standing, if ye dinna mind, Sir Oliver, Lady Margaret," Tavish replied. Her confidence returned. His tone of voice left no doubt who intended to direct the conversation.

"As you wish."

"First and foremost," Tavish began, looking into Piper's eyes, "I've come to ask for yer daughter's hand in marriage. I'm likely not yer first choice, but I promise to love and honor her all the days of my life."

The urge to rush into his embrace was powerful, but Piper had to trust her father to do the right thing.

"Aye, lad," Oliver Graham said, clamping a hand on Tavish's shoulder. "You'll do."

Only later would Piper recall her mother's stoic smile, her grandfather's whoop of approval, and Kenneth's enthusiastic applause.

All that mattered was Tavish's chaste kiss and the strength of his embrace as they came together. But she was thrown off balance by the hint of trouble lurking in his green eyes.

"Tavish is reluctant to tell you," Kenneth said. "An unforeseen problem has arisen. Actually, not really a problem, more of a complication."

Suddenly, there was no air in the room. What did he mean?

"The Regent might grant our distillery a royal warrant," Tavish explained.

Puzzled frowns and utter silence greeted this announcement until Piper's grandfather spoke. "Surely, 'tis good news."

"Aye," Tavish replied. "A grand honor beyond anything we ever imagined."

He proceeded to explain the summons to Carlton House and the Regent's delight upon tasting *Uachdaran*. "The Duke of Withenshawe was present. 'Twas he told His Majesty of the investment opportunity proposed by Kenneth."

"And the prince was in favor?" her father asked.

"Aye," Tavish replied with a sigh. "On one condition."

No one breathed. A thousand possibilities flitted

through Piper's brain, but she was gobsmacked when Tavish said, "He insists there should be no investment—and, by extension, no royal warrant—unless Withenshawe and any other potential investors travel to Glengeárr to see the operation for themselves."

LIFE IS UNPREDICTABLE

It took three weeks for the preparations to be completed. There was much discussion about who should make the trek to Glengeárr. Gregor refused to be left behind. Maureen absolutely insisted on going, and Kenneth had an obligation to evaluate the potential investment.

Tavish couldn't see the point of traveling home without his Piper. If she went, then her father and grandfather would also go. Margaret Graham refused to even consider making the long journey into what she referred to as *the back of beyond.*

Payton and Niven initially wanted to go home, but Withenshawe suggested they stay behind to liaise with the manager of his shipping empire. He was of the opinion that transporting large shipments of whisky by sea was the best option. Tavish had to agree, and his brothers were tasked with exploring this plan and finding warehouse space to store the shipments.

They were both enthusiastic about the assignments.

Tavish got the feeling Payton was especially glad to stay behind and suspected Jasmine Foxworthy had something to do with it.

Initially, three carriages were proposed for the journey, two courtesy of Withenshawe, and the other Kenneth's barouche.

Riders were sent ahead to arrange for fresh horses and accommodations at various coaching inns on the chosen route. Every piece of equipment was checked and rechecked from the carriage wheels to the tack to the horses' teeth, shoes and hooves. Halstead selected a team of drivers and guards for his carriages. Kenneth chose four men who'd worked for the Hawkins family for decades.

This flurry of excitement came to an abrupt end when it was decided that traveling by sea to Dundee would provide an obvious opportunity to test the waters, so to speak.

The plans for an intimate betrothal supper were shelved. Tavish was left with precious little time to spend with Piper. He called on the Grahams every afternoon, but Lady Margaret never left them alone together. He tried his best to engage the poker-faced woman in conversation but quickly realized he was never going to win her over. Piper deserved to share her happiness with her mother and he resented she'd been denied that rite of passage.

Three days before the planned departure date, he was surprised to be greeted at the door by an agitated Oliver Graham himself. Piper stood in the foyer, her eyes red, a kerchief clutched in her hand.

"What's amiss?" he asked, enfolding her in his arms.

"My wife has taken to her bed," Oliver murmured. "She claims she'd rather die than live with the shame of having an unmarried daughter go off to Scotland with a man."

Tavish recognized this as a ploy to thwart the marriage, but he saw a way to achieve his heart's desire. "'Tis easily remedied," he said. "Piper and I will marry before we leave."

His body rejoiced when a broad smile brightened Piper's face.

～

WAITING in the withdrawing room of Ramsay House for the bride to arrive, Kenneth mused on the unpredictability of life. He'd used his position as a duke to coerce a local minister to be present and offer a blessing from the Book of Common Prayer at a traditional Scottish hand-fasting. He stood next to the cousin who was about to pledge himself to the woman Kenneth had been wooing. He was rather proud of the fact he didn't feel an ounce of jealous resentment. Indeed, he was honored Tavish had asked him.

The event involved Scots, so there couldn't be a simple exchange of vows. Gregor had insisted a traditional hand-fasting couldn't hurt and would appease John Knox who must be turning over in his grave to see a Scot wed a Sassenach using only the Anglican liturgy.

Kenneth worried that he was actually beginning to understand his uncle's convoluted logic.

Only slightly more bothersome was his mother's enthusiasm. She looked stunningly beautiful in a gown of blue silk, her hair piled in an elaborate arrangement atop her head. She'd agreed wholeheartedly to witness the marriage. None of that troubled Kenneth. It was her obvious flirting with the other witness—Jock Graham. Even Gregor had argued against that choice and was glaring at the Lowlander. Kenneth wondered if his uncle's irritation perhaps had more to do with the undeniable attraction between Jock and his sister.

That possibility led to musings about what it was that attracted a man to a woman and vice versa.

The magic between Tavish and Miss Graham was plain to see, as was the chemistry between Jock and Kenneth's mother. Oliver Graham had absented himself to join his daughter, but it was painfully obvious that the pleasant fellow roused no such feelings in the sour-faced Margaret Graham. He felt very sorry for Graham. Had Kenneth married Priscilla, he too might have ended up with a bitter, resentful wife. The notion made him shiver. He'd had a lucky escape. Miss Graham made it clear from the outset she had no feelings for him, but he'd blindly ignored the obvious. Thank goodness Tavish had come along!

Kenneth had to hope that one day he'd find a woman who sparked his passion, something he'd never given much thought to before. He'd thus far considered it a duty to marry and sire heirs. Now, he wanted more than a dutiful wife. He wanted what he suddenly realized his parents had enjoyed. Passion.

"Good grief," he muttered under his breath. "You're beginning to sound like a Scot."

He pulled himself together when Tavish's radiant bride appeared in the doorway on her beaming father's arm.

BINDING

Tavish was the right man. Piper knew it for certain when he took her hand and she saw the sincerity in her proud Highlander's green eyes. She'd never dreamt she'd be marrying a man dressed in a kilt with a ceremonial dagger tucked into his Argyll sock. But there it was. She loved the magnificent Scot with an all-consuming passion. She took a deep breath to calm her frantic heart when the minister began the ceremony.

"The promises made today and the ties that bind here are meant to strengthen your union. Do you still seek to embark on this ceremony?"

"Aye," Tavish replied, his deep voice sending ripples of excitement swirling.

"Yes," she confirmed.

The familiar ritual began, the minister leading them in the age-old promises. Before finally declaring them man and wife, he turned to Gregor. "You may proceed," he intoned with great condescension.

Gregor bade everyone face the east as he raised his

arms. There was some confusion as to which direction was east, until everyone simply followed his lead, trusting he actually knew which way was east. "Blessed be this union with the gifts of the East and the element of Air, for openness and breath, and purity of the mind and body. From the East ye receive the gift of a new beginning."

Next, everyone turned with him without instruction. "Blessed be this union with the gifts of the South and the element of Fire, for passion and the warmth of a loving home. Share the fire within ye in even the darkest of times."

The fire within echoed in Piper's heart. She burned to lie abed naked exploring Tavish's tempting body.

"Blessed be this union with the gifts of the West, the element of Water, for yer ability to feel emotion. By hand-fasting, ye offer absolute trust to one another, and vow to keep yer hearts open in sorrow as well as joy."

Piper wasn't naive enough to believe she and Tavish wouldn't experience dark times, but they'd have love to sustain them.

"Blessed be this union with the gifts of the North, the element of Earth, which provides sustenance, fertility and security. The earth will feed and enrich ye, and help ye to build a loving home."

Aye, her heart proclaimed. A loving home, filled with Tavish's bairns.

She marveled that the old Scot had uttered these sacred words from the heart, not from a book. "Perfect," she whispered.

"Aye," Tavish replied hoarsely.

Gregor cleared his throat. "Tavish King and Priscilla Graham, I bid ye look into each other's eyes."

"I love ye," Tavish mouthed as they obeyed, his green eyes full of the love he professed.

"Will ye honor and respect one another, and seek to never stain that honor?"

"We will."

Gregor draped his plaid over their joined hands.

"And so, the first binding is made," he declared. "Will ye share each other's pain and seek to ease it?"

"We will."

Payton removed the plaid draped over his shoulder and placed it alongside Gregor's.

"And so, the second binding is made. Will ye share the burdens so that yer spirits may grow in this union?"

"We will."

Niven wound his plaid around their hands.

"And so, the third binding is made. Will ye share each other's laughter, and look for the brightness in life and the good in each other?"

"We will."

Lastly, Jock wound his plaid around their joined hands and knotted it loosely. She hoped her grandfather knew how glad she was he was present.

"And so, the fourth binding is made," Gregor declared. "Tavish and Piper, as yer hands are bound together now, so yer lives and spirits are joined in a union of love and trust. Above ye are the stars and below ye is the earth. Like the stars, yer love should be a source of light and, like the earth, a firm foundation from which to grow."

Eyes sparkling, Tavish pulled her to his body and they shared their first kiss as man and wife. There was nothing chaste about this kiss. Tavish's tongue took possession of her mouth. She melted into his hard body and willingly let him breathe for her. Raucous cheers and applause echoed in her heart.

∽

Tavish swore the vows from the Anglican liturgy with a true heart. He knew they were important to Piper. However, it was the hand-fasting that meant the most to him.

It wasn't the first time he had been present when his uncle conducted a hand-fasting. He'd never paid much attention to the sentiments before, nor to the reality that the cantankerous, unsentimental Gregor had committed the meaningful words to heart.

There was perhaps a side to this uncle he'd failed to appreciate. Was jealousy the reason he'd shunned his sister when she ran off with a lover? Had he too longed for a lass he could love?

At the outset of Gregor's litany, Tavish felt uncomfortable with the idea of *purity of the mind and body*. Heaven knew his body craved Piper—but his cravings weren't sinful. They were born of love. Wholesome.

Aye. There was fire within him and he couldn't wait to share the flames that threatened to consume him.

He admitted inwardly that he'd never trusted women, largely thanks to his unpredictable mother. In truth, he barely knew the lass he was marrying, but he trusted her implicitly.

He fully intended to provide Piper with sustenance and security and he prayed they'd bring many healthy bairns into the world—likely all redheads given their parents fiery locks!

These swirling thoughts flew away like a flock of startled birds when he kissed his bride—really kissed her for the first time. She melted into him and suckled his tongue. Oh, aye. Passion lurked in Piper King. His heart rejoiced that he was just the man to unleash it.

TO THE FUTURE

"I should mayhap ha'e worn my trews," Tavish teased as he placed Piper's hand on his thigh.

His bold behavior was well hidden by the tablecloth, but the warmth of his skin sent shivers up her spine. The wedding breakfast guests must surely have noticed her blush. "Why?" she asked, feigning ignorance of what she had an inkling lay mere inches from her fingertips.

"Minx," he replied, moving her hand slightly higher. "I wouldna want ye to mistake my sporran for..."

He stopped abruptly, probably because of the heat staining her cheeks. "I'm sorry," he whispered close to her ear. "I ken ye're a maid. I shouldna be talking to ye with such disrespect."

She smiled. He hadn't removed her hand from his thigh. She decided to meet his challenge by kneading her fingertips into his well-muscled leg. "I'm blushing because you're making me hot, husband. Not because I'm offended."

"Piper, lass," he growled low in his throat. "Let's hope we can escape this gatherin' soon."

"Aye, Tavish," she whispered in return, unable to look away from the fire burning in his emerald eyes.

He groaned when his uncle labored to his feet with the aid of his staff. "Gregor doesna ken the meanin' o' short and sweet."

"Be patient with him," she chided. "He loves you."

"Aye," he conceded. "Thinks he's my father."

"That's a good thing."

"Aye."

The wistful note in his voice told her he cared deeply for the crusty old man. Clutching his staff, Gregor swayed on his feet, clearly having difficulty getting started on his speech.

"What can I tell ye about Tavish King?" he began.

"A bossy *mon*," Payton shouted.

Polite laughter ensued.

"Aye," Gregor agreed sternly. "And a good thing too, else his naughty wee brothers woulda run amok."

More laughter.

Piper's heart swelled when Gregor narrowed his eyes at Tavish. "I'm prouder o' my nephew than I can tell ye. He's a fine, honorable man who makes the best whisky in the world. Ye've made a good choice, Piper Graham."

"Piper King now, Uncle," Niven pointed out.

"Aye," he replied hoarsely. "Ladies and Gentlemen, Lads and Lasses. Raise yer wee tumblers o' whisky and drink to the health of Tavish and Piper King."

As long as she lived, Piper would remember that smiling dukes, earls, family and friends raised their glasses in a genuinely hearty toast to her happiness. Even her mother took part, though Piper doubted she actually supped the tot of whisky.

Beneath her hand, a muscle twitched in Tavish's thigh.

∼

Tavish swallowed the lump in his throat. He knew how difficult it was for his uncle to voice his feelings. They'd never spoken aloud of their love for one another, and likely never would. But he thanked God for the man who'd taken the place of a miserable excuse for a father. The lives of the King brothers might have turned out very differently if Gregor hadn't taken them under his wing after Walter died. After Gregor regained his seat, he struggled to compose a reply to the toast, but Jock Graham rose to speak.

"Aye," Jock began. "Piper Graham is now Piper King. As her grandfather, I am delighted she's wed a man she loves and who loves her in equal measure."

His wife's fingers dug deeper into Tavish's thigh. "Keep that up," he whispered close to her ear, "and I'll be carrying ye upstairs afore Jock's done."

He regretted his teasing when tears welled in her eyes. "Sorry, my love. Ye've married a randy fool."

"What's even better," Jock added. "Tavish King is a Scotsman!"

Surprisingly, Aunty Maureen's unladylike whoop of approval was even louder than the cheers from Tavish's uncle and brothers. Lady Margaret's tentative smile fled.

"Now, English folk may not ken there's a certain animosity in Scotland twixt Highlanders and Lowlanders. I'm proud to be a Lowlander. Tavish calls the Highlands home, but Piper loves him, so I'm willing to overlook his geographic shortcomings!"

Hearty laughter greeted this jibe though it was likely that only the Highlanders present truly understood the rivalry that existed between people from the disparate regions of Scotland.

Jock raised his glass. "We've toasted the happy couple. Ye all ken that they're about to embark on a mission to make the King distillery world famous. Hopefully, ye've a wee drop o' single malt left in yer glasses to drink to the success o' *Uachdaran*."

"*Uachdaran*," echoed around the dining room.

His heart full, Tavish stood to respond. "Every Highlander's worst nightmare," he quipped. "Marrying into a family o' Lowlanders."

"Aye," Gregor shouted, but the jest was well received by his jovial audience.

"Seriously," Tavish added when calm was restored. "'Tis lamentably true I came to London seeking a bride, but I ne'er imagined I'd find a woman like Piper Graham. 'Tis rare these days for a man to find a woman he truly loves and who loves him in return. So, I consider myself the most fortunate o' men."

Risking a glance at his mother-in-law, he was surprised to see tears welling in her eyes. However, he was past caring if he offended the difficult woman or not. He scooped up his bride and declared, "Now, if ye'll excuse us, Piper and I have important business to attend to."

Loud cheers followed them as they left the dining room.

~

Maureen watched her nephew carry away his bride. Tavish and Piper were embarking on a journey through life's ups and downs. She wished them well and could only hope love would sustain them when things got difficult—as they surely would. She'd known there would be challenges when she ran away with Freddie Hawkins, but life as a duke and duchess had been more than challenging. Only their love for each other had helped them survive.

On the morrow, she was scheduled to board a ship bound for the country of her birth. Returning to the roots she had turned her back on was a holy pilgrimage—something she had to accomplish before she died.

She supposed making the journey to Scotland had always been in the back of her mind. Reuniting with Gregor had brought it to the fore and she was glad her brother would be there to support her as she revisited her past. Jock Graham would also be aboard the vessel. The excitement of that prospect had naught to do with the past.

WHAT'S UNDER A KILT?

It had been a good while, but Tavish had bedded women before. What red-blooded, healthy Highlander hadn't? However, in Glengeárr, only tarts slept with men and he'd never spilled his seed inside any of them. They weren't fit mothers in any case, and he had no wish to sire a brood of bastards. The lasses were a means to an end. He wasn't proud of his behavior, but needs must and it was the way things were for young men in the wilds of Scotland.

However, he was now married to an educated, refined woman. Peeling off his clothes in a big hurry and hopping into bed simply wouldn't do on this occasion. Plus, he wouldn't have the first idea how to unfasten a gown. His partners were usually undressed and in bed before him.

"You look nervous," Piper remarked as he set her on her feet inside the large guest chamber Kenneth had provided.

"Aye. That I am," he confessed, toeing off his boots.

She averted her gaze. "I was hoping...er...that is..."

This wasn't how he'd thought things would progress. He took her into his arms and pressed his needy manhood against her. "As ye can mayhap tell, 'tisna that I dinna want to bed ye. There's nay hurry."

Her puzzled frown and fierce blush told him she likely had no idea what he was talking about. Neither did he for that matter. He'd been hard since she'd first entered the drawing room on her father's arm. Going slow would be torture. He could beat around the bush all day and get nowhere—except embarrassed—so he decided to be direct. Unless he missed his guess, Piper would be a fast learner. He took a deep breath and guided her hand under his kilt to the intimate place he desperately wanted her to touch.

As he'd hoped, she curled her hand around him, looked into his eyes and growled his name. "I've been dying to know what's under this kilt," she teased, tugging at his belt with her free hand. "Let's get it off."

The MacGregor war-cry again seemed appropriate, but he could barely recall his own name as he let the kilt drop, tore off his doublet and shirt and spread his arms wide for her perusal.

He worried when her gaze fixed on his arousal. God had been generous with his physical endowments. She was a maid. However, he realized he'd married a playful lass who would fill his life with love and laughter when she quipped, "Will ye nay teck off yer socks, Tavish King?"

~

Piper wasn't sure what had come over her. She suddenly felt very Scottish! The sight of a broad chested, fully aroused Highlander clad in naught but his socks was enough to make any lass feel naughty! His laughter came as a relief, though he soon became serious again.

"This works better if we're both naked," he said. "I dinna ken much about removing a lass' clothes."

Piper wasn't naive enough to think her husband had come virgin to their marriage and she wondered about the kind of women he'd known. However, there was little point dwelling on the past. "There was no time to commission a complicated gown. You just need to help untie the laces," she replied, turning her back to him.

He nuzzled her neck as he worked to free her.

"I didn't wear a corset. To make things easier."

Icy heat flooded her veins when he eased the frock off her shoulders and kissed her back through the thin fabric of her chemise.

"Ye smell wonderful," he rasped, reaching to cup her breasts as the bodice fell to her waist. "I've longed to hold ye in my hands."

The gown pooled at her feet when she pushed it off over her hips. Growling, he lifted the chemise over her head, scooped her up and carried her to the bed. Kneeling between her legs, he meshed his fingers with hers, stretched her arms above her head and loomed over her.

"You've a naughty glint in your eyes, Husband," she teased, her body flooded by arousing sensations when he bent his head and licked a nipple. "Oh," she gasped when the licking turned to suckling.

She tangled her fingers in his long hair as he feasted on each breast in turn. "I feel wicked in a very private place," she admitted, not the least bit embarrassed to make such an intimate confession to a man she'd known only a few weeks.

When he opened her legs and shifted his attention to the part of her body she'd never seen, her absolute trust wavered only momentarily. She hadn't known men tasted their wives, but quickly understood the appeal as rapture built to a crescendo. His clever tongue found one particular spot that..."Tavish," she screamed as she tumbled into an abyss of bliss, barely able to breathe.

"Aye, lass," he replied hoarsely. "Ye're ready for me now."

∾

TAVISH HELD Piper tightly as he lunged home. She cried out when he breached her maidenhead. Gooseflesh marched across her heated skin. "The pain will pass, *mo ghràdh*," he promised, struggling to hold still.

"I didn't think you'd fit," she gasped.

"Oh, aye, we fit together perfectly," he replied. "Yer body will get used to me."

His heart rejoiced when her hips slowly began to move in the age-old rhythm.

"Feels better already," she said.

He ought to assure her that the best was yet to come, but his loins demanded all his attention. She was tighter even than he'd expected and his cock reveled in the warmth of her pulsating sheath as he thrust. He was sweating by the time his seed erupted from his body and carried him into rapture. Her cry of ecstasy robbed him of breath. They'd soared to heaven together.

SETTING SAIL

The day after the wedding, everyone bound for Scotland assembled their luggage in the foyer. The remaining King brothers and Daisy intended to see them off. There was no sign of Lady Graham. Kenneth privately thought it cruel of her not to show up to bid farewell to a newly married daughter whom she might never see again.

Kenneth took Tavish and Piper aside. He had more bad news to impart. "I want to apologize in advance," he told them. "It wasn't up to me. Withenshawe owns the ship and he decided on the allotment of cabin space."

Tavish nodded. "We had a feeling we wouldn't get to share a cabin."

Piper agreed. "Since your mother and I are the only two women, I assumed I would be sharing with her."

"That is the case," Kenneth replied. "And I'm sorry."

The newlyweds held hands and seemed resigned to being parted for the voyage. Kenneth prayed there might come a day when a beautiful woman would look at him with such longing.

Dismissing the distraction, he forced his attention back to the matter at hand. "Listen, everyone," he announced. "Withenshawe has given me a list of cabin assignments. Tavish will bunk with Uncle Gregor, Jock and Oliver Graham are together, Piper is with my mother, and I'm with Halstead himself."

"I suppose the two dukes have the best cabin," Gregor groused.

Kenneth ignored him. "Our ship awaits," he shouted.

In the driveway, Payton, Niven and Daisy hugged the travelers and wished them Godspeed.

The carriages previously intended for the road journey transported the seagoing adventurers across London to the docks.

~

"Impressive," Jock declared when he first saw Withenshawe's schooner from the windswept dock.

"Four masts," Oliver remarked before wandering off to help direct the luggage.

"Bigger than I expected," Maureen replied.

Detecting a hint of fear in her voice, Jock took a risk and reached for her hand. "This vessel makes the voyage north regularly. We'll be in Dundee before ye ken it."

"I know. It's simply that I've never been aboard a ship before."

She hadn't withdrawn her hand, which he took as a good omen. "Piper will be good company."

"She will, though I'm sorry she cannot share a cabin with her new husband."

"Aye, and I'm sorry I hafta share wi' my son. He snores mightily!"

Maureen laughed. "Well, you'd have the same problem if you shared with me."

She blushed profusely and studied the wooden planking as soon as she realized the implication of what she'd said.

Jock decided nothing ventured, nothing gained. "If I shared a cabin wi' ye, Maureen Hawkins, ye wouldna be sleeping long enough to snore."

She looked up sharply. For a moment he feared she might slap his face, but then she smiled coyly. "You're a bad lad, Jock Graham."

His sense that she had amorous feelings for him had been correct. "This journey might turn out to be more than just an investigation of a good investment," he whispered.

"Aye," she agreed. "Though I'm sure Piper is glad you're coming along since her mother hasn't deigned to see her off to her new life."

He filled his lungs, hoping the air would be fresher once they left the Thames behind. "What to say about that? Margaret Graham's an unforgiving woman."

∼

"Gregor was probably right," the Dowager Duchess said. "The cabin my son is sharing with Halstead is likely much bigger than this cupboard."

Piper eyed the small bunk bed tucked into one corner. She and Tavish could have happily made do, but obviously she couldn't cuddle up with Maureen Hawkins.

"One o' yous can use this."

They hadn't realized the sailor who'd guided them still stood in the doorway, attaching the end of a piece of fabric to a hook in the wall.

"A hammock!" Maureen exclaimed. "I think not."

The scruffy, malodorous fellow shrugged, dropped the hammock and let the door slam as he left.

"I'll sleep in the hammock," Piper said. "It'll be an adventure."

"It's to be hoped that sweaty wretch never slept in it," Maureen replied. "Not the honeymoon you imagined, I'll warrant. Sleeping alone in a hammock."

"No, but it's just for a week or so until we arrive at Glengeárr."

"A week can seem like an eternity when you're longing to be with someone."

Piper understood that only too well but didn't want to sound like a spoiled child. "Not much to be done about the situation."

She expected the Dowager to agree, but the woman tapped her chin and said, "You never know."

They were startled by a loud banging on the door. "Piper, ye must come," Tavish shouted.

Elated, Piper thrust open the door. Her hopes plummeted when she saw the stern set of her husband's jaw. "What's amiss?"

Shaking his head, he took her hand. "Yer mother. Best ye come up on deck."

~

Gathering her skirts, Maureen followed Tavish and Piper up the companionway, thought she had difficulty keeping up with their pace.

On deck, she joined her son and others looking across at the dock, startled to see Margaret Graham teetering on the edge.

Piper sobbed against her husband's chest.

Jock and Oliver were urging men to replace the gangway that had been removed in preparation for departure.

"What's happening?" she asked Kenneth.

"The lady's threatening to jump."

"Why?" she asked, though she suspected Margaret had lost her wits and likely didn't understand her actions.

"She'll drown herself if Piper and Oliver abandon her."

Maureen gripped her son's arm as she watched Jock and Oliver finally lope down the repositioned gangway. Just as they reached the dock, Margaret swayed and fell into the filthy water.

"No," Piper screamed when her father stripped off his frock coat and jumped in to rescue his wife.

Moments later, Maureen gathered Piper into her arms and prayed as they watched Tavish, Kenneth, Oliver and Jock dive to search the mirky waters.

DRYING OFF

His clothing sopping wet, Tavish shivered, reminded of his unpleasant arrival in Edinburgh. He gulped air, glad he'd worn his trews and not his kilt.

He enfolded Piper in the blanket a sailor threw around his shoulders. She clung to him, clearly not caring about getting wet.

"Get ye to our cabin," Gregor commanded.

"No," Aunty Maureen contradicted. "Fetch his dry clothing to our cabin."

"But..."

They left Gregor spluttering as his aunty hustled them away to the cabin she shared with Piper.

"Get him out of those wet clothes."

Her tone of voice seemed to jolt Piper from her trance. Tavish nodded and she helped him shrug off his jacket. "Forgive me, Yer Grace," he said.

"Nothing to forgive," she replied. "I'm leaving to see

to the others who were fool enough to risk their lives for that thoughtless woman."

Anxious to protect Piper's feelings, Tavish bristled. "That's…"

"Ye ken I'm right. You could all have drowned, leaving this poor lass an orphaned widow and me a grieving mother."

Having apparently recovered her wits, Piper carried on helping Tavish to remove his apparel until he was clad in just his trews. "I'd be obliged if ye'd turn yer back, Yer Grace," he growled.

"No need. I'm off. Once I'm assured Kenneth is all right, I'll go see Jock. He has a cabin to himself since Oliver has to stay behind to take care of his selfish wife."

Moments after she'd left, Gregor arrived, scowling at the sight of Piper rubbing warmth back into Tavish's limbs.

"Dinna fash," Tavish told him. "Piper's my wife."

"But where's my sister? This is her cabin."

"Gone to administer aid to the others," Piper replied.

"Others?"

"Kenneth…and my grandfather."

"The woman's lost her wits," he exclaimed as he bolted for the door.

Piper chuckled. "I believe he just figured out that my grandfather now has a cabin of his own."

He was relieved to see her smile again after the ordeal. "Do ye want to stay in London? Help nurse yer mother?"

"No, Husband," she replied. "My place is with you."

Kenneth would never admit his Uncle Gregor was right about the furnishings of the cabin he was to share with Withenshawe. Not only was it spacious, the accommodation came with the services of a valet. Langford had him out of his wet clothing, scrubbed dry and dressed in less than ten minutes—which was just as well because his mother burst in without knocking.

"You're dressed," she exclaimed.

It was on the tip of his tongue to tease her with a ribald remark, but the valet already looked offended. "Yes, thanks to Langford here."

"You have a valet?"

"He's Withenshawe's servant."

She eyed him curiously. He had a suspicion she'd rush off to tell her brother he'd been right about the dukes having more amenities. Perhaps her Scottish side was getting the better of her usual sense of decorum.

"I wanted to make sure you were all right," she said. "And I see you are in good hands."

"Where are you off to?" he asked as she opened the door.

"Piper is taking care of Tavish, so I thought I'd check on Jock."

It took him a few minutes after she'd left to realize Jock Graham was no longer sharing a cabin with his unfortunate son. He dismissed Langford and waited until he was sure the man was well away before exclaiming, "Bloody hell!"

Assailed by doubt, Maureen dithered outside Jock's cabin. What if he was still undressed? What if he didn't have feelings for her? What if...

"*Crivvens*, woman. Do you want the man or not?"

Her heart threatened to burst out of her chest when the door was thrust open.

"I hoped ye'd come," Jock said, smiling as he pulled her inside.

Did she dare?

Aye!

"And I hoped I could help ye change. But here ye are, fully clothed."

"We can soon remedy that," he replied, gathering her into his arms.

She leaned into his solid strength. "I felt powerless and afraid watching people I care about struggle against the tide and a demented woman."

"Aye. I warned Oliver long ago that the marriage wouldna work. Bitterness has stolen Margaret's wits."

"I'm glad Piper and Tavish married. I thought she was the right woman for Kenneth, but I was wrong."

"Aye, a relationship canna be successful unless both people feel the magic."

"Is magic what we have, Jock?"

"Definitely, Maureen lass. Ye've bewitched me."

AT SEA

As the schooner made its way through choppy seas, Gregor's turmoil grew. It turned out he wasn't a good sailor. His appetite fled and he retched up most of what he did eat.

He lay the blame for his malaise on his sister.

On the one hand, he was pleased Tavish and Piper were together for the voyage. A newly married man shouldn't be separated from his bride. He was also glad to have a cabin to himself, especially given his queasy belly.

On the other hand, his sister's consorting with Jock Graham stuck in his craw and did naught to alleviate his malady.

After the first day at sea, he avoided the galley. No one else seemed to have been afflicted with seasickness. Engrossed in each other, Tavish and Piper ate ravenously —no doubt refueling the fires!

Jock and Maureen sat apart for meals, but Gregor wasn't fooled. Did she think he didn't know she'd moved into the Lowlander's cabin? The smug smiles she sent in his direction infuriated him all the more. Was she daring him to chastise her?

Kenneth must also be aware of what was going on, yet he chatted amiably with his mother and with Jock as if naught were amiss.

Gregor lay awake in his bunk at night, wrestling with his anger. He'd alienated Maureen before and seemed intent on doing it again. "Ye're just a judgmental *auld* fool," he confessed to the shadows. "Small wonder ye ne'er found a woman who'd put up wi' ye."

∽

"I know it's wicked of me," Maureen confessed to Jock as she lay in his arms in the narrow bunk. "But I'm enjoying taunting Gregor."

"I'm surprised he hasna punched me," he replied. "Same wi' yer son."

"I'm not certain what to think of Kenneth's behavior."

"Mayhap he's glad to see ye happy."

She mulled over what he'd said. "I am content when I'm with you."

"No feelings o' guilt?"

"None. I loved Freddie, but he died and I didn't. What about you?"

"Same. Maddie's gone, but she'd want me to be happy."

"Besides, we haven't yet done anything to feel guilty

about. There's nothing wrong with kissing and cuddling."

He remained silent for a while, then said, "Right. But, sooner or later, we'll both want more."

Years of marriage to a man she loved had taught Maureen a great deal about the male body. Jock hadn't pushed, but she recognized the signs of arousal. "I already do," she admitted. "And you've been more than patient."

"I'm a patient man, but my patience isna endless. I want ye."

"And you shall have me—eventually."

She hadn't lied when she declared she didn't feel guilty. So, what was holding her back?

∽

On the third night at sea, Kenneth lay awake, staring into the creaking beams above his bunk. The cabin was more spacious and boasted better amenities. But Withenshawe snored like a pig.

He'd tossed and turned every night, though the noise wasn't the only reason. He wasn't sure how he felt about his mother's philandering.

Perhaps that was the wrong word, and who was he to sit in judgment? The *ton* couldn't know what went on aboard a vessel at sea. The reputation of the Ramsay dukedom was safe. His mother had been a loving and faithful wife to his late father and been largely instrumental in establishing his stellar standing as a duke. There was definitely an attraction between her and Jock. Kenneth had learned a lot about amorous feelings thanks to Piper Graham. Strange how he naturally thought of her as Piper now.

Several times during the sleepless nights, he'd been on the point of retreating to Gregor's cabin. He'd get no sleep there either. His uncle no doubt disapproved of his sister's behavior and would harangue him about it.

It came to him that he would defend his mother's choice. Life was too short to spend it alone. Maureen Hawkins deserved every bit of happiness Jock could give her.

Then why did his belly churn every time he thought of his mother in bed with the Scot?

∼

Wishing he could stay inside Piper forever, Tavish accepted the inevitable when his sated cock curled up at her entry. He'd lost count of the number of times they'd made love since the Dowager Duchess had left them alone to enjoy the cabin three days ago. He couldn't get enough of his wife, and her desire for him seemed insatiable. Her passion had done wonders for his male pride.

However, he was a big man and the bunk wasn't built for two people. "I've been selfish," he said, relishing the touch of her fingertips tracing circles on his back. "I'll sleep in yon hammock tonight and leave ye in peace."

"You'll do no such thing, Tavish King," she retorted. "I intend never to sleep alone again."

"Weel, if ye insist," he replied, turning her so she lay atop him. They'd slept every night in the same position and he loved to feel her completely relax on top of him. She'd been embarrassed about drooling on his neck, but he loved that too.

He'd never been happier, but they hadn't yet talked about what awaited them in Glengeárr. The King family's ancestral home was a far cry from what she was used to. He'd have to prepare her before she saw the ancient house he shared with his brothers—and his uncle.

This would be their last night together. Aunty Maureen had suggested it would be better to revert to the original cabin assignments on final night of the voyage.

DUNDEE

By the time everyone disembarked in the port of Dundee, Withenshawe's dock laborers stationed there had two carriages ready and waiting to take them to Glengeárr. "I suppose there's advantages to travelin' wi' two dukes," Gregor muttered to Tavish.

"Aye. More comfortable than our wagon."

"You came from Glengeárr in a wagon?" Piper asked.

"Aye," Gregor replied. "Rained the whole way and we'd only a tarpaulin to shelter us at night."

Tavish clenched his jaw when the color drained from Piper's face. Time was running out for him to prepare her for the new reality of living in the Highlands, and Gregor's wagging tongue wasn't helping. "I hafta be honest," he said. "Things are different here. You'll nay find it easy."

Gregor rubbed his hands together. "But Withenshawe has arranged an inn for tonight so we'll nay be sleeping outdoors," he exclaimed gleefully.

"I didn't realize it was so far to our home," Piper murmured.

Gregor nodded. "Weel, Dundee's at least closer than Edinburgh, though the road might be just as bad."

Tavish groaned inwardly. "Dinna fash," he said. "These carriages look sturdy and we'll be home by the morrow."

"Aye," Gregor confirmed. "Payton and Niven are still in London, so ye'll only ha'e me to put up wi'."

"You live in the same house?" she asked, her amethyst eyes wide as saucers.

"Aye," Gregor replied sheepishly, scurrying away abruptly.

"He just realized he's revealed too much, hasn't he?" she said.

Tavish took hold of her hand, hoping to make amends. "I'm sorry. I should have told ye before this. I was afraid ye might change yer mind about…"

She touched a fingertip to his lips. "I can get along with Gregor. At least with him I can be direct. I couldn't get my own mother to listen to me."

The knot in his gut loosened. "I dinna deserve ye," he whispered, too much of a coward to tell her about Glengeárr's other drawbacks.

∼

Piper's grandfather lived in Galloway, further south than Tavish's Highlands. She'd visited him there and was well aware living in Scotland wasn't the same as London.

She hadn't anticipated sharing a house with Tavish's

uncle and brothers, but the prospect wasn't overwhelming. Scots kept their families close and she ought to have taken that into consideration.

Life was simpler in Galloway—harsher in a way, but she'd often found London overly sophisticated. Upper class Londoners were too concerned with societal expectations. Scots were down to earth and had good reason to be resentful of the English. More than fifty years had passed since the fateful Battle of Culloden but the memory of the horrific aftermath haunted even Lowlanders like her grandfather. The Highlands had suffered far worse vengeful cruelty at the hands of the Hanoverian regime. That was worrisome. Would the people of Glengeárr welcome her or would she always be an outsider, an enemy?

The irony was inescapable. If Margaret and Oliver Graham had loved each other, they might have stayed in Scotland and she'd have been born there, instead of in London.

Despite the location of her birth, deep in her heart, she recognized she had more Scottish blood in her veins than English. That reality, and Tavish's love, would hopefully see her through whatever trials lay ahead.

∽

Tavish's return to the cabin they were supposed to share alerted Gregor to the fact Maureen had gone back to Piper's cabin for the last night of the voyage. Determined not to be usurped by Jock Graham, he made his way there as soon as the ship docked. He let his sister know in no uncertain terms he intended to be the man who escorted her when she stepped ashore in Scotland.

Her immediate enthusiastic approval of the idea banished his anxiety. Their fledgling reconciliation was still in place.

"I've ne'er set foot in Dundee afore this," he admitted after they disembarked and were boarding the second of Withenshawe's carriages.

"Neither have I," she confessed. "But I could tell right off that we're in Scotland. Even the air is different, but the rich twang of the dock workers' speech confirmed it."

"Aye. I'm glad Tavish and his bride ha'e gone ahead with the dukes."

"I think the news you live in the same house as Tavish may have shocked Piper," his sister replied as they settled into the plush squabs.

"Aye. Me and my big mouth," he conceded. "'Tis obvious Tavish hasna prepared his new wife for what's in store."

He bristled when the carriage lurched. It couldn't be...

"Prepared her for what?" Jock asked as he boarded and made himself comfortable beside Maureen.

Gregor had thought the Lowlander had gone in the first vehicle, yet here he was, glaring at Gregor as if he were the interloper. "Graham," he growled.

Maureen chuckled. "You lads had best learn how to get along, especially if we are all going to live in the same small community for a wee while. Gregor's referring to the fact the King's ancestral home isn't what Piper is used to."

"Dinna worry about my granddaughter. Scottish blood runs in her veins. She'll adapt."

"Wait," Maureen said. "I just realized what you said. If you live with the lads, does that mean...?

"Aye," Gregor confirmed reluctantly. "The house we grew up in has been closed for two years. There was only me left in the place, and Tavish invited me to live wi' him and his brothers."

"So, where will Jock and I be staying?"

Gregor had thought his sister could take one of the lads' rooms, but he hadn't given a thought to accommodating Jock, nor to the two dukes. "I suppose there's always *The Crow and Gate*," he suggested.

"They have rooms there now? It used to be a place where only heavy drinkers congregated."

"Nay. It's fairly posh these days," he lied.

~

KENNETH HESITATED to bring up the question of accommodations in Glengeárr. "Do you have a place to stay lined up for all of us?" he asked Tavish, realizing belatedly he ought to have tasked Mainwaring with the arrangements.

The uncertainty on his cousin's face was worrisome, but Withenshawe came to the rescue. "Don't concern yourself with us," he declared. "I had a pavilion shipped up. My men should have erected it by now. Lots of room for Mr. Graham too and all the comforts of home."

Kenneth breathed again, but it struck him there was

so much more he could achieve as a duke. Withenshawe would be a good role model.

"A pavilion!" Piper exclaimed. "Sounds like something my grandfather will enjoy."

"And Aunty Maureen can stay wi' us," Tavish said. "The house she grew up in has been closed up for a wee while now."

That news would disappoint his mother. "I believe she'd like to see it, though," Kenneth said. "As would I, for that matter."

"I'm certain Gregor will arrange it," Tavish assured him.

TAXES

"'Twas generous o' Withenshawe to provide us wi' our own room," Tavish said.

Piper cuddled into her husband. As always, she'd enjoyed the intimacy they'd shared in *The Last Drop's* cozy bedchamber. They were learning to prolong each other's pleasure and intensify the rapture. However, she sensed Tavish was preoccupied. "I don't expect to live in luxury," she told him, hoping to allay his fears.

He lifted her so she was lying atop him. She loved falling asleep this way, but he seemed restless this night.

"Trust me," he replied. "My home doesna offer much in the way o' luxury. But 'tis comfortable and warm and, most important of all, 'tis waterproof!"

"We'll be happy there," she declared.

"Aye. Ye're my happiness, Piper."

"So, stop worrying."

"I'm sorry. My mind's on a matter I need to discuss wi' Kenneth."

This news came as a surprise. "Kenneth?"

"Aye. Ye see, our distillery isna licensed. Most distilleries in the Highlands balk at paying taxes to the Hanoverian Crown."

"But if the Prince Regent grants a royal warrant..."

"Exactly. However, we're tenants o' the Earl o' Craigdarroch. So far, it seems we havena come to his notice. He'd have to grant the license."

"Kenneth and Withenshawe's endorsement will surely carry weight?"

"Craigdarroch's an unpredictable fellow. I heard tell he turfed out some tenants who've lived on his land for generations. Wants to clear the fields for sheep rearin'."

∽

Tavish agreed with his wife that it would be preferable to discuss the licensing problem with Kenneth before they actually arrived in Glengeárr. Withenshawe had arranged for breakfast to be served in a private dining room for him and his traveling companions. Everyone was seated by the time Tavish and Piper arrived. It was mildly amusing to see Gregor was sitting between Piper's grandfather and Aunty Maureen. He was engaged in lively conversation with his sister, his back turned to Jock. Tavish wished he'd had a chance to discuss the licensing with his uncle, but it was now or never, and never wasn't an option.

"Ah, genuine Scottish oatmeal," Maureen declared with delight when a steaming bowl was served to each guest.

"Aye," Gregor replied after sampling a spoonful. "Wait till we get home. My oatmeal puts this to shame."

"Pity we'll not have the chance to sample it," Withenshawe remarked. "My cook will be providing our meals."

"Let me explain," Kenneth said in response to the puzzled frowns. "Halstead here has arranged for a pavilion where he, Jock and I can camp out."

This news came as a relief. Tavish had tried and failed to sort out the problem of where everyone would sleep.

"And Maureen can stay at the big house wi' us," Gregor declared with a grin. "And we've been discussing maybe openin' up the old house, just for a wee while."

"I'd certainly like to see the house where my Lockie ancestors grew up," Kenneth added, smiling at his mother.

"As would I," Jock said, earning a scowl from Gregor.

"Yes," Aunty replied. "I didn't realize it had been closed up. We'll have to tend to making it habitable again."

Tavish could readily see the advantage of Gregor moving back into his old home, but it sounded like Aunty Maureen was planning on staying in the Highlands indefinitely. He deemed it a good opportunity to bring up the topic of their landlord.

∽

Maureen listened intently to Tavish's explanation about Craigdarroch and the licensing issue. She remembered the earl only too well. Even as a young viscount, he'd been a miserly fellow. She could only imagine what a curmudgeon he was now—probably well into his eighties.

However, as a duchess, she had learned to handle crotchety men who thought their title gave them the right to ride roughshod over ordinary people.

"Aye," Jock replied in answer to Tavish's reasons for not paying the tax. "'Tisna so easy for Lowland whisky distillers to evade the government tax collectors, and they resent having to pay when Highlanders dinna."

"Well," Maureen interjected. "Obviously, we'll have to obtain a license and pay the taxes if we want the Regent's blessing. If needs be, I'll deal with Craigdarroch."

"Ramsay and I will help twist his arm," Withenshawe promised.

∽

Tavish breathed more easily. Everyone was talking as though the investment were a foregone conclusion. Piper relaxed her painful grip on his thigh, but her touch had already worked its magic.

He wasn't looking forward to spending a few more hours in the cramped carriage, prevented from touching the woman he craved constantly.

In the event, he was spared the torment when Withenshawe proposed he, Kenneth, Gregor and Tavish travel together in order to plan how to proceed.

Gregor sulked, probably because the arrangement

left Jock in the other carriage with Aunty Maureen. The sparkle in her eyes indicated she was happy about that, although Tavish suspected she resented being left out of the discussions. He regretted Piper's deep pout.

"I wanted us to be together when we reach Glengeárr," she confessed.

"Me too. But I intend to carry my bride o'er the threshold o' her new home," he replied. "I'm confident ye and my aunty will get busy making plans o' yer own. And ye'll be wi' yer grandad."

"Too bad the duke didn't think to include him. He's a canny fellow with a wealth of experience in business."

Too preoccupied with Margaret Graham's antagonistic behavior, Tavish had been remiss in not learning more about Piper's family. He tucked away the tidbit of information concerning her grandfather.

THE PALACE

After navigating laneways and rutted grassy tracks for hours, the carriage came to a halt in a field in the middle of nowhere. Certain she must be covered in bruises, Piper looked out of the window to see her husband jump down from beside the driver of the lead carriage. "I wonder why we've stopped here?" she asked.

"If I have my bearings correct," Tavish's aunty replied, "we're not far from the distillery."

Tavish opened the door and held out his hand. "Yonder *Lùchairt*. Let's walk the rest of the way."

"*Lùchairt?*"

"Tavish's ancestor had visions of grandeur," Maureen explained. "It's Gaelic for *palace*. What else would a man named King call his dwelling?"

Tavish chuckled. "Weel, 'tisna a palace, but 'tis my bonny wife's new home and I want her to see all our wee domain."

Catching sight of a roof and chimneys off in the

distance, she accepted his hand and stepped down from the vehicle. She loved the unmistakable pride in his voice. The red apples were back in his cheeks. The wind toyed with his auburn hair. She closed her eyes to store up the memory of a heartwarming milestone in her life that she would never forget.

Still holding her hand, Tavish led the way. "We grow most of our barley in these fields. We harvested the crop before we left, so it looks barren at the moment."

"Except for the wildflowers that have taken advantage," Piper replied, charmed by the swathes of color waving in the gentle breeze. "Do you grow all your own barley?"

"Mostly, though we might have to start buying more from our neighbors if we expand our market. They'll be pleased about that."

They drew closer to the house. It was bigger than she expected. "Two stories," she exclaimed. "And three chimneys."

"Aye. Highland winters can be brutal, but ye'll be toasty warm. We've a hearth in our bedroom. The other two fireplaces are downstairs. The distillery needs a constant supply o' peat, so we ne'er run short."

Visions of making love in front of a cozy fire danced in Piper's head.

Tavish's voice jolted her back to the tour. "The original distillery was built as an outbuilding," he told her. "As ye can see, the numerous additions have resulted in it coming right up close to the house."

"More convenient, I'd think," she replied, impressed

by the size of the distillery and the number of workers scurrying about here and there.

"I'll introduce ye to the crew later, after we get settled," he said.

"Good idea. I don't look my best after days of traveling."

"They'll be gobsmacked by yer beauty and wonder how a coarse fellow like me managed to wed a lass like ye."

The welcome flattery resulted in a long kiss. She was engrossed in suckling his tongue, until she noticed a large red and white striped tent off to the side of the distillery. "What's that?"

He squinted at the structure. "Must be Withenshawe's pavilion," he replied, shaking his head. "Apparently had it brought by ship from America. He told me this is its first big test."

"I'm glad there'll just be me and you in the house."

"Dinna forget my aunty and uncle."

"I know, but I suspect they'll be busy with their own reunion."

She pulled Tavish to a halt just before they reached the house. "I want to take it all in," she said, her eyes roving over the solid stone construction, the five large windows downstairs and the two dormers jutting out from the roof. "I can't wait to see the inside."

His smile fled. "Just bear in mind four bachelors have lived here for a long while. We've neglected Mam's kitchen garden and ye'll likely want to fix that. Now, ready?"

He scooped her up and kicked open the blue door.

Heart fluttering, she clung to his neck. It was impossible not to notice the peeling paint and the stern set of his jaw. She'd warrant there'd be more to fix than the kitchen garden and she couldn't wait to get started.

∼

THE FIRST THING Tavish noticed was the smell—or rather the absence of odors he supposed he'd got used to. He'd expected Piper to wrinkle her pretty nose, but she inhaled deeply and smiled. Somebody had been hard at work tidying up and polishing furniture—even Gregor's rickety rocker had a shine to it. The smoke-blackened walls sported fresh whitewash. The aroma of burning peat wafted from the fire in the brick fireplace whose bricks were no longer black. A vase or two held cut lupins. He barely recognized his own home, but he was grateful and suspected he had Auld Jamie's granddaughter to thank for the transformation.

"You're surprised," Piper said as he set her down in the parlor.

He might have known his clever wife would notice his puzzled frown. "Aye. We've a lass comes in to cook. Catriona's the granddaughter of our wagon driver. Looks like she did some housecleaning while we were away."

"Good of her," she replied, one brow arched.

"Dinna fash," he assured her. "If anything, Cat's sweet on Payton, nay me."

"Then we'd best not tell her about Jasmine Foxworthy."

"I suppose ye're right. Now, are ye ready to see our bedroom, Mrs. King?"

The promised intimacy of the moment was spoiled by Gregor's voice at the front door. "Later, *mo ghràdh*," Tavish growled.

∼

MAUREEN WAS PLEASANTLY surprised by the cleanliness of *Lùchairt*. Gregor looked equally amazed, so she surmised someone must have been in to clean up in the lads' absence.

It was strange to enter this house where her sister had come as a bride and apparently lived an unhappy life. By contrast, Gregor had uttered dire warnings about her future if she ran away with Freddie. In fact, she'd been blessed with a very happy marriage and lived in the lap of luxury. She expected to feel Moira and Walter's presence, but didn't. She was glad for the brothers' sakes that their parents didn't haunt the place.

Voices from another part of the house indicated Tavish was showing Piper her new home.

"They're in the kitchen," Gregor explained.

"Is that your rocker?" she asked her brother.

He looked at the chair as if he'd never seen it before, but replied, "Aye. Sit in it, if ye like."

She rocked back and forth for a few minutes, worried she might fall asleep as exhaustion swept over her. "It was a long journey," she murmured.

"Aye, but 'tis grand to see ye here again. On the morrow, we'll walk over to Lockie House."

"Grand," she echoed as her eyelids fluttered closed.

～

Jock would have preferred to follow Maureen into the house, but he had a feeling Gregor would resent his presence and, when a duke offers accommodation...

The pavilion he'd been invited to share with Ramsay and Withenshawe was worthy of any Bedouin prince.

"You say you had this brought by ship from America?" Ramsay asked, clearly as impressed as Jock as he ran his gaze over the opulent furnishings.

"Say what you will about the colonials. They know how to do things in style," Withenshawe replied.

Three men who had lined up just inside the entry bowed.

"Our cook and his assistants," Withenshawe explained with a dismissive wave of his elegant hand.

The superior attitude of the upper class had always rankled, so Jock shook each man's hand in turn and introduced himself. "From Galloway," he added.

Wide eyes betrayed their surprise at his gesture and the mention of Galloway elicited a hint of a snigger.

"How long before the meal is ready, Frobisher?" Withenshawe asked, cutting off any further opportunity for conversation.

"An hour at most, Yer Grace."

"Good. And sufficient food for our guests, let's see, seven of us in all."

"Aye, Yer Grace."

Frobisher toddled off and the duke instructed the

other two to show his guests to their chambers. They might have been in a mansion instead of what amounted to a tent in the Highlands.

"Typical toffs," Jock muttered. "Must keep up appearances no matter what."

FINE DINING

Piper stared at what Tavish had told her was a wood-stove. She'd never actually visited the kitchens at Graham House, so had no way of knowing if her family's cooks produced meals on a similar piece of equipment. Even if they did, she had no idea how to go about making a meal on such a primitive-looking apparatus. She supposed a wood-stove burned wood, but...

"I'm not a good cook," she confessed to her husband. "Not a cook at all, for that matter."

"Dinna fash," he replied. "We've got used to doin' fer ourselves. Gregor's a fair-to-middling' cook and Catriona can teach ye."

Piper had insisted she was ready for anything the Highlands could throw at her, but had to admit she'd never considered what the lack of servants really entailed. "I hope I don't let you down," she murmured.

"Of course you won't let him down," Maureen said as she appeared in the kitchen. "And we don't have to worry about meals while Withenshawe is here. He's invited us all to dine in his pavilion. I nodded off but his man woke me up when he came to let us know."

"But after the duke's gone..."

Tavish's aunty shrugged. "Mam used to cook hearty meals on a hearth stove. We'll tackle this monster together."

Piper found it humbling that the Dowager Duchess was more supportive and encouraging than her own mother.

"Aye," Gregor agreed when he joined them. "'Tis easy, once ye get the hang o' the beast..."

∽

"THIS IS posher than the dining room at *The White Horse*," Gregor remarked to Tavish as Withenshawe's servants cleared away the dishes. "Better food too."

Tavish agreed, but he'd be just as glad when he could eat ordinary food in his own home. This show of opulence and wealth was all a bit too much. He was nervous about his workers in the distillery. "Auld Jamie and the others must wonder what's afoot."

"I had a word on the way here," his uncle assured him. "The duke's lackeys had already told part of the tale, and they are keen to meet Piper."

Seated next to Tavish, his wife sighed. "I trust you didn't build up their hopes about me."

"Dinna concern yerself. They'll love ye," Gregor replied.

"Aye," Tavish confirmed. "But do they understand

that our visitors are considering investing in the distillery?"

"They do. Auld Jamie'll make sure all's in order on the morrow. The men are excited about wearin' their Sunday best to work."

Kenneth leaned over to join the conversation. "Understandable. Expansion means secure employment and good wages."

Tavish had to trust that the two dukes wouldn't renege on their commitment now they'd come so far. He was confident a tour of the well-run operation would seal the deal. There remained only the problem of the Earl of Craigdarroch.

～

Maureen made a big show of dabbing her mouth with the linen napkin. "This is all to the good," she whispered to Jock.

"Ye mean fine dining in a tent in the middle o' nowhere?" he replied.

"Wheest, man, keep yer voice down. Can ye no see yer granddaughter is overwhelmed?"

"Now, ye sound like a Scotswoman! But what does one thing have to do wi' t' other?"

"Coming back here has made me realize I've always been a Scotswoman, but that's beside the point. We need to make Piper understand that finer things can exist even in the middle of nowhere. She won't always have to deal with primitive conditions."

He frowned. "The house is that bad, is it?"

"No. It's clean, well furnished and spacious, but the kitchen is a nightmare. The lads probably don't realize it, but I saw the horror on Piper's face."

"I doubt she has any experience cookin' in any case," he agreed, rubbing his chin. "I dinna believe she's the kind o' lass who wants to live in the lap of luxury, else she'd ne'er have agreed to come north."

Maureen nodded. "However, things can be improved and she has to believe that. Expanding the whisky business will result in Tavish spending long hours working. Piper will have to learn to cope on her own."

"Aye. I suppose I've been lookin' at Piper's new life here through a man's eyes. I'm glad ye came along too."

"And I'm glad you're here," she replied, though *glad* seemed a paltry word for her burgeoning feelings for the Lowlander.

∼

KENNETH COULDN'T SHAKE the vague feeling that things weren't as they should be. He'd certainly enjoyed the roast lamb and the rest of the tasty meal prepared by his fellow duke's servants. He had no idea how they'd managed such a feat in the middle of nowhere. Therein lay his malaise. Was it the Scot in him that felt this show of wealth was out of place here in the remote glen where his ancestors had lived?

He suspected from the set of Tavish's jaw that he was equally uncomfortable with the lavishness. He'd originally thought he had absolutely nothing in common with his Scottish cousin, but perhaps they weren't so different after all.

His mother was her usual refined self, but he suspected she couldn't wait to see her old home on the morrow. He was looking forward to it with more anticipation than he would have believed possible. There was something about Glengeárr that had already seeped into his blood and it wasn't the comfy amenities of the pavilion, nor the roasted lamb.

LIGHT MY FIRE

It was dark by the time Tavish and Piper set off to walk the short distance to the house. Gregor and Tavish's aunty followed a little way behind. The biggest full moon Piper had ever seen lit their way. She filled her lungs before they went inside. "The air smells different here," she remarked.

"Aye, fresher than in London," he replied. "Plus ye can probably detect the aromas o' peat and malting barley from the distillery."

"The smell of success."

"We hope so."

Bothered by the hint of doubt in his voice, she held him back to let their companions enter the house first. "I know there's a great deal riding on the investment, but you've already proven your whisky is superior. Withenshawe wouldn't be here otherwise and the Regent wouldn't be dangling the possibility of a royal warrant."

"I suppose ye're right," he agreed. "Ye and me are

from different worlds. 'Tis important ye understand what *Uachdaran* means to me."

He didn't mean to hurt her feelings but his words were nevertheless hurtful. "You can't believe I think less of you because you're not of noble birth. Of course I understand that whisky is your passion. I'll work hard to be your equal in this endeavor."

He drew her into his arms and kissed the top of her head. "Whisky was my only passion, until a certain Piper came along and I fell head o'er heels in love wi' the saucy lass."

The moment was ripe for one of her husband's mind-boggling kisses, but they startled when the door creaked open.

"Are ye plannin' to stay out here all night?" Gregor asked. "I've lit a candle to light our way upstairs if ye've a mind to come in."

Tavish chuckled. "Our bower awaits, Mrs. King. Are ye ready?"

"Aye," she replied, though her heart was fluttering wildly. They'd made love before, but she was about to finally see the bedroom they would share for their entire lives together.

Gregor and his sister had already embarked on the stairs when they entered. "Impatient as ever," Tavish said. "He's nervous about showing aunty to her room. 'Tis where my brothers usually sleep. They moved in together so Gregor has his own room."

"That's generous of them to share."

He shrugged. "Else-wise they'd get no sleep. Uncle

snores. Payton and Niven aren't known for being tidy. Let's hope Cat's efforts extended to upstairs."

Piper selfishly hoped the same thing, although there was something unsettling about an unknown female having free rein in her husband's home. She had no time to think further on the matter when Tavish scooped her up, carried her further down the narrow hallway and kicked open a door.

It was dark enough to hide the fact she closed her eyes. Relying solely on her sense of smell proved to be for the best. She knew instantly this was where her husband slept. Tavish King's spicy masculine scent lingered. She inhaled deeply. Everything was going to be all right.

~

Tavish was relieved only the moonlight illuminated his bedroom. He'd never noticed before that the space seemed stark and unwelcoming. Perhaps Piper hadn't noticed.

Then Gregor trundled in and lit a candle on the mantelpiece. "There ye go," he declared with a wink before leaving.

It was then Tavish saw the colorful patchwork eiderdown on the bed. He stared at it, until Piper whispered, "You can put me down now."

"I dinna ken why I'm so nervous," he confessed as he set her down.

"It's understandable. You've probably had this room to yourself for many years. This is lovely," she said running a hand over the eiderdown.

How to tell her it must belong to Catriona? Then she might think...

"I've ne'er brought a woman here," he said, deciding they had to begin life together with honesty. "But the counterpane is Cat's. 'Tisna mine."

"That was thoughtful of her," his wife replied, turning down the linens. "I must thank her for the clean sheets too when I meet her."

"Aye," he replied, beyond grateful that he detected no jealousy in Piper's voice. "I couldna be sure if I made the bed before I left."

She sidled over to him seductively and put her arms around his neck. "So, are we going to christen our bedroom tonight?"

"Oh, aye, lass," he replied, pressing her against his needy body. "I feared I might burst watching ye lick the juices off yer fingers during the meal."

"I did it on purpose," she confessed with a naughty grin. "I like teasing you."

"Minx," he exclaimed as the tension eased from his shoulders. His wife was exactly where she belonged.

∽

Piper and Tavish made quick work of undressing in the chilly room and dove into bed. "These sheets are like ice," she exclaimed.

He gathered her close and rubbed her back. The heat from his body chased away the chill. "How can you be so warm?" she demanded. "I'm freezing."

"Would ye like me to get up and light the fire?" he asked.

"Don't you dare leave this bed," she replied. "You can light my fire right here."

"I intend to," he growled.

As they began the slow climb to ecstasy, touching and pleasuring each other, Piper forgot all about the chill in the room. The iron bedstead creaked in tandem with Tavish's thrusts, but she didn't care. The lovemaking was as intense as it had been from the start, but this time was special. They were joining their bodies in their own home, in the bed where, God willing, Tavish would plant the seed of the next generation in her womb.

As she soared on clouds of rapture, Piper knew she had never been happier. She was where she belonged.

THE TOUR

Gregor could be as irritating as a cocklebur, but Tavish was glad his uncle intended to be present during the all-important tour of the distillery. He missed his brothers. They'd been a team for as long as he could remember. Payton and Niven could provide information he might forget to mention, but Gregor would keep things on an even keel.

Piper was right. There was no reason to be nervous. If the investors reneged and the Regent changed his mind, it would be their loss and certainly wouldn't be because *Uachdaran* wasn't the finest whisky to be found anywhere. Tavish already had the most important thing in life—the love and support of a beautiful and passionate woman who'd given up a great deal to live with him and enrich his life.

"Ready, gentlemen?" he asked the visitors milling around outside the pavilion. He immediately realized his mistake. His aunty had joined the group.

"Lead on," Withenshawe replied, seemingly oblivious to the slight.

Tavish proffered an arm. "Allow me, Aunty," he said, hoping to make amends.

Smiling sweetly, she linked arms with Piper's grandfather. "I'll walk with Jock. You need to be free to concentrate on explaining the process to these *gentlemen*."

He nodded to acknowledge he deserved the jibe, then led the way into the distillery.

"I'm surprised Piper isna here," Jock remarked.

Tavish's bride had begged to be included in the tour but, selfishly, he wanted the two of them to be alone together when she first toured the distillery. There were little things he was proud of that he didn't intend to share with the others. "I'll show her everything later," he replied.

"First off," he began with an expansive wave of the hand. "The barley is steeped in water. Then, as ye see here, 'tis spread out on the malting floor to sprout shoots."

Withenshawe and Kenneth huddled beside the malting barley, hands behind their backs. Tavish suddenly didn't care what they were discussing in hushed tones. He was king of this domain. They were fools if they didn't see its worth.

He led them to the kiln where he explained, "'Tis then baked in a kiln to dry it out before 'tis milled. We burn peat to dry the malted barley. This gives our whisky its smoky flavor."

His visitors inhaled deeply and closed their eyes. The peat was working its magic.

"I understand ye turn the malt by hand during this process," Jock said. "Is that unusual?"

Tavish silently thanked Piper's grandfather for mentioning an important detail he'd forgotten. Maybe he was getting too cocky. "Aye. 'Tis hard work but the malt absorbs more of the peaty aroma. We turn it every eight hours, seven days a week."

"Somebody must have kept up the good work in your absence," Withenshawe observed.

Tavish was glad several of his workers were quietly going about their duties as if a group of well-dressed foreigners toured the distillery on a daily basis. He was used to seeing them in overalls. They looked incongruous in their Sunday best but, typical of Scots, they stayed unobtrusive in the background. "Aye, we've a skilled crew here. Many of our workers have been with us for decades."

"Aye," his aunty replied. "I recognize some of them."

"A reliable workforce is paramount," Withenshawe stated. "And they don't object to working for a younger man?"

Gregor snorted. "Tavish is a master of his craft. He's well respected in the glen."

It occurred to Tavish that perhaps he should have allowed Piper to come along!

He ushered the group over to the mash tun. "The barley, or *grist*, is mixed with hot water in this contraption known as the *mash tun*. A sugary liquid called *wort* is produced. We make the whisky from this liquid. The leftover solids are used as cattle feed—nothing goes to waste."

"Capital!" Kenneth exclaimed.

"Moving on. The liquid wort is passed into the large vats ye see here. We call them *washbacks*. Yeast is added and allowed to ferment which converts the sugars in the wort into alcohol. This liquid is now known as the *wash*.

"Next comes the best part," he declared as the visitors stared at the two huge copper stills. "The liquid wash is heated in these pot stills. The vapor rises and is collected and poured into oak casks to age."

"Why two stills?" Withenshawe asked.

"We distill single malt twice," Tavish replied. "Then 'tis stored in the cellar 'neath yer feet."

"For how long?" Kenneth asked.

"At least three years. We've some that have been in the cellar since my father's day."

"Can't wait to taste that," Withenshawe exclaimed.

"We could try it now, if ye wish, but I was thinkin' to treat the Regent to that vintage—if he carries through wi' a royal warrant."

"He's a canny lad, my nephew," Maureen declared with a proud grin.

"Indeed," Kenneth echoed.

Tavish's hopes rose.

"One more thing. Ye ken we sent staves to Spain. The Spaniards made them into barrels and they've been used to age sherry there for nigh on three years."

"'Tis agreed we'd get them back," Gregor explained. "But we need coin to accomplish that."

"What's the thinking about aging your whisky in these sherry barrels?" Kenneth wanted to know.

"Weel," Tavish replied. "Only time will tell, but I

believe 'twill make *Uachdaran* the finest whisky in the world. Now, all this talkin' has made me a mite thirsty. Let's away to the cellar and see what we can find to whet our parched throats."

He didn't have to tell them twice.

∼

AFTER TAVISH LEFT to conduct the tour, Piper stayed in bed and sulked for a while. She understood why her husband wanted to give her a private tour, but felt left out and abandoned nevertheless.

Wide awake despite having spent half the night making love, she sat up and contemplated the curtains. "Definitely need replacing," she muttered. "Probably put up by Tavish's mum."

She'd never been good at sewing but how difficult could it be to make curtains? An idea struck her when she ran a hand over the eiderdown. If Catriona had made it...

She startled when a door slammed downstairs, followed by a hearty, "Hellooo."

Catriona!

"I'll be down directly," she shouted, leaping out of bed. Gooseflesh ran rampant over her naked limbs. She could not allow Tavish's Cat see her looking like a ravaged wanton.

That thought made her chuckle. Prim and proper Piper Graham had indeed become a wanton.

She searched desperately for the chemise thrown to the four corners last night. She shivered when the icy cold silk molded to her body but it was nothing to the shock of realizing that a raven-haired beauty stood in the open doorway, hands on hips like a wild gypsy.

"Seems ye could use a hand," Catriona said, entering without so much as a *by your leave*.

"Er..."

"I'm Cat," the woman said, retrieving Piper's gown from the floor and shaking out the creases.

"Pi..Piper," she stammered. "Tavish's wife."

"Assumed as much," Cat replied with a wry smile. "He's a lucky man."

There was no hint of jealousy or resentment in Cat's voice. "I would appreciate your help," Piper confessed. "I'm useless at dressing myself."

Could she sound more like a spoiled noblewoman?

"I meant..."

"I ken what ye meant. Dinna fash. Me and my sisters helped each other dress until they married and moved away. 'Tisna a bother."

Piper began to hope she'd found a friend. "The eiderdown is lovely. Thank you."

"Ye're welcome. Ye ken how men are. Nay notion of the things that are important to women. None o' the brothers had e'en made the bed. Just up and away to London. And dinna get me started on their grumpy uncle."

Cat chattered on as she assisted Piper to prepare for a day that suddenly held promise.

NEGOTIATIONS

Tavish had envisioned negotiations taking place amid the comfortable splendor of the pavilion, but supposed the cellar beneath the distillery was perhaps the most appropriate place.

He pointed out the oldest barrels, but no one pushed for them to be tapped. Instead, he'd apparently won them over with samples of five-year-old *Uachdaran*.

Kenneth asked about the bottles they used. "I see *Uachdaran* is formed right into the glass."

"A glass blower in Edinburgh makes them specially for us," Tavish replied. He'd boast about his role in securing that contract to Piper, but these gentlemen didn't need the details.

"So," Withenshawe began after downing his third glass. "Ramsay and I intend to jointly invest 1000 pounds, plus I offer the use of my ships at no charge for a period of five years."

The amount of money alone was beyond Tavish's

most optimistic hopes, but the Scot in him sensed the dukes wanted something in return for their generosity. It was tempting to reply immediately, but he waited.

"We give you free rein to spend the money how you see fit," Kenneth went on. "However, we expect to receive sixpence for every pint distilled."

Tavish did some quick thinking. If Craigdarroch granted the license, he'd be paying two shillings tax for every pint. Add sixpence on top of that...

It seemed churlish to haggle, but what kind of Scotsman would he be if...

"Thrupence a pint," Gregor declared before Tavish had a chance to speak. "Nay a penny more."

Tavish's cousin and his fellow duke exchanged a glance before Kenneth offered his hand. "You drive a hard bargain, Uncle," he said. "Three pennies for every pint."

"'Tis a deal," Tavish agreed, shaking Kenneth's hand first, then Withenshawe's.

◈

When Withenshawe invited everyone to a celebration in the pavilion, Maureen huffed. It was typical of men that they thought the conclusion of their business dealings brought matters to a close.

"Patience, *leannan*," Jock whispered close to her ear. "Let me do the talkin'."

Maureen had learned to be patient with arrogant noblemen, but being addressed as Jock's *sweetheart* convinced her he was right.

"A moment before we leave, if ye please, Yer Graces," he said.

Withenshawe pouted.

Jock ignored him. "Tavish, being the gentleman ye are, ye've ne'er mentioned yer bride's dowry."

Maureen feared Jock may have taken the wrong approach when her nephew bristled. "I dinna need a dowry."

"But ye are aware I arranged for Piper to receive a small inheritance of two hundred pounds from me when she came of age, or when she married."

"Best ye discuss that wi' my wife," Tavish replied angrily.

"Of course. I simply want to tell ye I dinna object if she thinks to invest in the distillery."

Snorts of derision from both dukes were a sure sign they thought that women couldn't be trusted with money. Maureen intended to have a serious talk with her son after this. For now, she was content to make her move. "I believe Piper would be proud to invest in her husband's venture, as would I. *Uachdaran* merits two hundred pounds, and I invest it in memory of my sister, Moira."

"And ye can count me among yer investors," Jock declared. "Two hundred pounds for the love ye've shown my granddaughter. No strings attached."

∼

PIPER WAS ENJOYING a delicious bowl of oatmeal prepared by Cat when Tavish burst into the house. Things had gone well if the broad smile and red cheeks were any indication.

"Cat made my breakfast," she began, noting he hadn't seemed surprised to see her new friend. Indeed, she wondered if he'd noticed Cat at all.

"Ye'll ne'er believe the money they've pledged," he exclaimed, taking her into his arms when she got up from the table. "And free use o' Withenshawe's ships for five years. Then there's the other investors who expressed interest after the tasting. Withenshawe thinks they'll come on board once he meets with them on his return."

When Cat whooped her glee, he turned his attention to the wood-stove. "Cat," he said. "I didna see ye there."

"Both dukes invested?" Piper asked, smugly satisfied to have it confirmed that Cat wasn't her rival.

"Aye, and my aunty and yer grandfather as well."

"Then I want to invest my inheritance," she declared. "I'll speak to my grandsire."

"He already gave his blessing if ye want to invest in the business. But ye havena seen how we operate yet."

"I'm investing in you, Tavish."

Desire smoldered in his eyes. His arousal pressed against her mons. Breasts tingling, she melted into him. This was a momentous occasion to celebrate upstairs, but a loud cough jolted them back to reality.

"When is Payton comin' home?" Cat demanded, the wooden spoon clenched in her hand.

"Er...I dinna ken," he replied. "I almost forgot. Food awaits us in the pavilion when ye're both ready to go."

TAVISH SEEKS A WEALTHY BRIDE

"I say, Withenshawe," Kenneth declared. "These are the best olives I've ever tasted."

"Kalamata. Imported from Greece," came the reply.

"And the cheese?" Kenneth asked.

"Closer to home. Lancashire."

"Delicious!"

After uttering this last expression of appreciation for the hors d'oeuvres, Kenneth made the mistake of looking to the opening of the pavilion just as he popped another olive into his mouth. It went down whole, stone and all, when he set eyes on a raven-haired gypsy who entered with Tavish and Piper.

If he had any lingering worries about his body's ability to respond to a beautiful woman, it disappeared like dust in the wind when his manhood came to full salute. Unfortunately, the olive lodged in his throat had him gasping for breath. An embarrassing coughing fit ensued which only ended when Withenshawe thumped him on the back and he spat out the olive.

Gulping air, he wiped away tears and risked another glance at Piper's companion. He wasn't certain what to make of the amused expression on her face. However, the choking experience hadn't dampened his male enthusiasm.

He followed in Tavish's wake as the beauty was introduced to his mother. Her name was Cat. His cock purred its approval, until his mother said, "You're Auld Jamie's granddaughter. I remember him. Is he here?"

Of course she was a commoner. Kenneth had never felt more bereft in his life.

EVICTION

Withenshawe suggested it would be appropriate for the distillery workers to be present when papers were signed the day after the momentous agreement. Tavish was pleased to have them as witnesses to events that would have a significant effect on their own lives. If the Regent gave his blessing as a result of the endorsement of these investors, the whole glen would benefit from the expansion of the distillery.

Words of wisdom and platitudes in speeches from both English dukes were received with polite applause. A rousing cheer greeted the news Jock Graham had invested, accompanied, of course, by remarks from the locals about it not mattering a whit that he was a Lowlander.

However, the announcement that Dowager Duchess Maureen Hawkins had invested in memory of her sister produced the loudest cheer of all. Tavish wasn't surprised the applause brought tears to his aunty's eyes, but the workers had never shown much respect toward his bad tempered mother. He sensed their affection was for Aunty Maureen herself.

He was perplexed by the absence of Auld Jamie and Cat. It wasn't like them to miss such an important occasion. He mentioned it to Piper, who shared his concern.

Silence fell over the noisy crowd when a breathless Cat burst into the pavilion, her face streaked with tears.

Tavish hurried to her side, but Kenneth got there first. "What's amiss, dear girl?" Ramsay asked, taking the distraught lass by the arm.

"Bailiffs," she cried. "Come to evict Grandad and me."

"On whose authority?" Tavish demanded, though he had his suspicions.

"Robert Dunsmuir, the cursed Earl of Craigdarroch," she sobbed against Kenneth's shoulder. "They're doin' the rounds of all the cottages in the glen."

Her warning resulted in an exodus as workers rushed away to return to their families.

"Where's yer Grandad?" Tavish asked.

"Gone to plead his case at Craigdarroch, though he says 'twill do no good, so he took his pistol."

"Right," Kenneth declared. "Tell your ostler to get the carriage prepared, Withenshawe. Without workers we can't run this distillery. His Highness won't be pleased."

"I'll come with ye to point the way," Tavish said, hugging Piper tightly in an effort to reassure her. If Craigdarroch intended to clear the glen, he wouldn't hesitate to oust the King family. Piper had entrusted her life to him. He couldn't allow his landlord to destroy what generations of his family had built. Perhaps he should search for his father's pistol.

"Why not take a bottle or two of *Uachdaran*?" Piper suggested.

Her question calmed his agitation. "Clever lass," he replied.

∽

KENNETH HATED LEAVING CAT, but his mother would take care of her. He'd never felt such a sense of outrage, nor such a fierce need to protect a woman. But it was simply because she was a damsel in distress, and he...well...he was her knight in shining armor!

Thoughts of how he'd look in one of the suits of armor in Ramsey House's gallery elicited a chuckle.

"This is no laughing matter," Withenshawe exclaimed. "Here we are speeding hell for leather in a carriage to confront a fellow nobleman neither of us have ever met."

"My mother remembers him from when he was a young viscount," Kenneth replied. "A snobbish tyrant was how she described him."

"Aye," Tavish added. "He's reputed to be a hard man. Let's hope this crate o' my whisky will soften him."

"Well, it worked with Prinny," Withenshawe remarked.

Kenneth sat back against the squabs and tried to calm his agitation. He would never be so callous as to summarily evict lifelong tenants from Ramsay lands. His anger gradually ebbed as the miles flew by, but his manhood refused to let go of the memory of Cat's body clinging to his as she sobbed.

His brain told him his attraction was foolhardy, but his loins paid no mind.

His emotions were in knots by the time the carriage clattered into the cobblestone courtyard of Craigdarroch Castle an hour later.

~

Tavish seethed. He was in the Highlands, a place he'd lived and worked all his life. For generations, his family had paid rents to the landed gentry. Yet, in this situation, his opinions and the welfare of his family and his workers would count for nought if Craigdarroch decided to be stubborn. It was the social standing of two titled Englishmen that might carry the day—and, ironically enough, their connection to a Hanoverian prince.

But he had a secret weapon—his beloved *Uachdaran*. He was all for hefting the crate into the castle, but Withenshawe advised against it.

As soon as Withenshawe introduced himself and Kenneth to the porter, the portcullis was raised. "Medieval," Kenneth muttered as they were led along endless narrow corridors to a sitting room and instructed to wait. Tavish's cousin had been in a foul mood throughout the journey, but he was right about their surroundings. Shields, pikestaffs and swords adorned the wood-paneled walls. An enormous black iron chandelier hung from the ceiling. Kenneth's sulk worsened when he caught sight of suit of armor standing in one corner. Tavish had never seen his affable cousin in such a bad humor. Confrontation loomed, which, from what he'd heard of Craigdarroch, didn't bode well.

He was taken aback when a middle-aged man entered. His clothing bespoke wealth and he reeked of entitlement. After a sneering glance at Tavish's kilt, he addressed himself to the two dukes. "Viscount Dalwhinnie," he said nasally. Tavish would lay odds he'd received his education at an English Public school. Probably Harrow. Eton would turn up its nose at a Scot.

There was no offer of a handshake nor any mention of his guests' titles. Kenneth bristled visibly and looked ready to unleash a stream of vitriol, but, thankfully, Withenshawe spoke first. "William Halstead, Duke of Withenshawe," he announced, extending a hand. "And may I introduce Kenneth Hawkins, Duke of Ramsay and his cousin, Tavish King."

Dalwhinnie had no choice but to shake hands with all three visitors and was politically savvy enough to mutter, *Your Grace* to Halstead and Kenneth. To Tavish, he merely said, "King." It was all Tavish could do to keep a straight face when the pompous fellow scowled upon realizing what he'd said.

"We came to see the earl," Withenshawe explained calmly. "We have a business proposition."

"I'm afraid my father is bedridden. I handle his business affairs."

Withenshawe arched a brow, but took this news in stride. "May we be seated and discuss the matter with you?"

"What's it concerning?" Dalwhinnie asked, casually

waving them to a settee. It was big enough for two to sit comfortably, so Tavish preferred to remain on his feet.

"The distillery at Glengeárr."

"I heard there was a distillery there. In fact, my father is rather partial to the whisky they produce."

Tavish's hopes rose.

"However, when I say partial, I mean he has drunk himself into ill health. Hence, I never touch a drop of the stuff. In any case, we plan to clear the whole glen for sheep. Good profits to be made in wool these days, but you English chaps are likely aware of that already."

DALWHINNIE

Kenneth found Dalwhinnie's attitude insulting and cruel. Not just for Tavish's sake, but for all Scots who were at the mercy of unfeeling landlords who considered sheep more important than people. The Scottish blood boiled in his veins, and it was for his mother that he determined to get the better of this poor excuse for a nobleman. "Aye," he replied, deliberately making it clear he had a personal stake in this matter, not just a financial commitment. "We make a fair profit on our wool, and sheep are relatively easy to manage. Shepherds are content with low wages, although we're obliged to provide them with shelter, as ye might expect."

"Of course," Dalwhinnie replied.

The hesitation in his voice implied he hadn't given a thought to that bothersome detail.

"Then there's the greater expense of shipping the wool overseas. Tricky with Napoleon on the loose. Withenshawe here owns a fleet of ships so he can tell ye about that."

"Indeed," Withenshawe agreed.

Dalwhinnie had remained standing but he shifted his weight from one foot to the other. "Er...I was under the impression you were an English duke, Ramsay, but I detect a hint of a brogue."

"Aye, English as ye say. Educated at Eton and Oxford. But my mother hales from Glengeárr, so I have a personal interest in the well-being of its people."

"That's how Mr. King comes to be your cousin."

Satisfied he'd put Dalwhinnie in his place and planted seeds of doubt about sheep-rearing, Kenneth ignored the hint of a smile tugging at the corners of Withenshawe's mouth and carried on. "If ye granted the King distillery a license, I dare say the tax of two shillings per pint o'whisky distilled would far outweigh any profits from sheep, and entail no work at all on your part. Sheer profit."

Dalwhinnie's eyes widened. "And how many pints of whisky are we speaking of?"

"Weel, at the moment, Tavish here produces mainly for the glen and other parts o' Scotland, but he's already secured several major wealthy investors, myself included.

"Can ye credit my brilliant cousin plans to age his whisky in sherry barrels imported from Spain? Imagine what that'll do to enhance the flavor."

The viscount licked his lips.

"And once the Regent grants a Royal Warrant...."

The color drained from Dalwhinnie's face. "A Royal Warrant?"

"Aye, like yer father, our good friend, Prinny, kens a superior whisky when he tastes it. He'll nay be best pleased if his supply is cut off."

"Indeed," Withenshawe repeated.

"So...er...you mentioned a license."

"Aye," Tavish replied. "Ye grant the license and I'm obliged to pay ye two shillings tax on every pint."

"Consider it granted. You'll have the paperwork within the week."

"One other minor thing," Kenneth interjected. "The Kings canna operate the distillery without workers. If ye evict his workforce..."

"Yes, yes," Dalwhinnie replied. "All cancelled. Is there perchance still an opportunity to invest?"

∽

Tavish could hardly contain his glee. The prospect of the Craigdarroch estate investing in his distillery was beyond belief, especially if, as he claimed, Dalwhinnie wasn't a whisky drinker.

But Tavish had seen him lick his lips.

Teetotaler, my arse.

"I dinna wish to offend, my lord, but I'd be honored if ye'd accept a bottle or two o' *Uachdaran*. Mayhap for yer father to enjoy a wee drop now and again. I can fetch it from the carriage while ye discuss investment wi' my cousin. He's a better head for business. I'm just a simple Highlander."

"Capital idea," Dalwhinnie replied.

Tavish chuckled as he made his way back to the courtyard, hoping he didn't get lost in the maze of corridors.

He'd brought six bottles but had no intention of leaving them all for Dalwhinnie. They'd need the rest for a wee celebration on the return journey.

∽

CAT AND PIPER kept each other company while the men were gone. Gregor had taken his sister and Piper's grandfather to see what could be done to open up the family homestead. Nobody mentioned that would be futile if the land were cleared of dwellings.

Piper didn't really know what to say to a woman under threat of being cast out of her home and whose grandfather had gone off with a deadly weapon. She couldn't rid herself of the ball of dread lodged in her belly. If the earl wanted to clear the whole glen he might evict the Kings from the distillery. Her grandfather would take them in, but Tavish would be devastated. *Uachdaran* was his life and their future.

For want of a better topic of conversation, she mentioned replacing the curtains in the house. Then they moved on to an explanation of how Cat had fashioned the eiderdown. She wanted Tavish and Piper to keep it as a wedding gift, so they spent a few minutes arguing good-naturedly about that.

Piper was at her wits' end when they finally heard

the carriage return. Hoping for the best, she and Cat held hands as they left the house.

Tavish, Kenneth, Withenshawe and Auld Jamie tumbled out of the conveyance and held on to each other, clearly having difficulty remaining upright. "They're three sheets to the wind," Cat declared. "And what's Grandad doin' in the carriage?"

Piper hadn't known what to expect, but a drunken husband wasn't it. Either all was lost or…

"Catriona," Auld Jamie bellowed, waving his pistol. "Dinna fash. I didna kill Craigdarroch."

Piper nigh on swooned when her grandfather appeared on the scene and wrenched the weapon from Auld Jamie. "Careful, ye might hurt somebody wi' that."

The other three drunken fools thought this drama was hysterically funny, until Tavish's breathless aunty arrived and stared at them, hands on hips. "What's the meaning of this?" she demanded, sounding every inch like a Dowager Duchess.

"We came 'cross Auld Jamie on the way back," Kenneth explained. "So he didna need to shoot Craigdarroch."

"Who's verra poorly, by the way," Tavish added, a silly grin upon his face. "Yon earl, that is."

The dowager folded her arms across her chest and tapped her foot. "Kenneth, did ye get the license or nay?"

Her son sobered. "Aye, and Dalwhinnie wanted to invest in the distillery. So, we proposed free rent as his contribution."

His sober demeanor was apparently too much for his companions who again snorted their laughter.

"And," Auld Jamie announced. "All evictions are cancelled. His lordship's gone off the idea o' sheep."

Piper had no idea who Dalwhinnie was but she and Cat embraced each other, laughing until they cried tears of relief.

SLEEPLESS

Withenshawe hosted a splendid celebratory dinner in the pavilion after the triumphant return from Craigdarroch. The drunken victors lost some of their hubris as they gradually sobered up. Cat eventually woke her dozing grandfather and took him home. Gregor escorted Piper and Maureen back to the house.

Jock was elated and relieved his granddaughter's future had been secured, but his thoughts wandered elsewhere as the men told and retold the tale of Dalwhinnie.

He couldn't deny his growing feelings for Maureen Hawkins. The prospect of returning to Galloway without her didn't sit well in his gut. She'd already confided her intention to stay in the Highlands for the time being. She'd cried during the visit to her former home earlier in the day. He understood and was smugly pleased when she turned to him for solace and not her brother. The Lockie house clearly held all kinds of memories—good and bad. It was a solid, spacious dwelling and he agreed with the two siblings that it wouldn't take much to make it habitable again.

Was it folly to imagine himself living there with her?

Gregor would likely have his guts for garters if he suggested it.

∾

MAUREEN AGREED with whoever had said Gregor snored like a circus bear. She could hear him in the next room. However, it wasn't the noise that was keeping her awake.

It had been an exhausting day full of highs and lows. The home where she'd grown up was in better shape than she'd expected, though the threat of eviction hung over them throughout the inspection. Now that problem had been resolved, she could give full consideration to reopening the house and living out the rest of her life there.

The Dower House in London was a lonely place. She would miss Kenneth but he was a capable man who had his own busy life. Eventually, he would marry and have children. Daisy too would build a life of her own. She might even agree to come north.

In Glengeárr, Maureen would have Gregor for company and could lend a hand to her nephews as their business expanded. She'd invested money, so they could hardly say nay.

If only she had the courage to ask Jock to stay in the Highlands with her.

Gregor might burst into flames if she suggested it.

~

Kenneth couldn't sleep. Probably the aftereffects of consuming too much whisky, though his mother's decision to stay in the Highlands played on his mind. He wasn't surprised. The place had a way of pulling a person in. If it weren't for his responsibilities to the dukedom, he might consider staying himself.

Then he and Cat could...

"Bollocks!" he growled, annoyed with himself for even thinking he and Jamie's granddaughter could have a future.

The sooner he returned to London, the sooner he could resume his life and forget all about a raven-haired Scottish lass.

~

Gregor sat bolt upright in bed, startled awake by his own snoring. After the day's events, he was surprised he'd slept at all. He was delighted his sister wanted to reopen the Lockie family home and live there with him. He appreciated his nephews offering him a roof over his head, but Tavish was married now. He and Piper didn't need an old codger about the place. Brother and sister could spend the last years of their lives having a grand time. He'd work hard to atone for his cruel treatment of her thirty years ago.

As much as he'd rather avoid the subject, he had to give some consideration to Jock Graham. Maureen couldn't hide her feelings for the man and he was obviously smitten with her.

For a Lowlander, Graham wasn't a bad chap.

It was likely nothing would come of their relationship. They'd both be reluctant to suggest Jock stay in the Highlands and live with them. Strangely, he found no solace in that outcome.

~

Piper lay awake, her mind filled with a chaotic jumble of thoughts.

Earlier in the day, it seemed her life might fall apart. Now, the future looked bright.

She understood why Tavish had wanted to stay in the pavilion after she left. He'd apologized for over-imbibing. She wasn't upset about it. He and his stalwart investors deserved to celebrate their victory. Whisky was Tavish's life, but he wasn't a man driven to drink to excess.

However, she missed him in her bed. She'd never shared a bed with anyone, now it was impossible to sleep alone.

She wondered about Maureen Hawkins' decision to reopen the family homestead and stay in the Highlands. Kenneth had tried to hide his initial reaction to the news, but it was obvious from his frown that he had doubts.

Mind you, his nervousness around Cat was even more curious. Throughout his brief courtship of Piper, he'd never shown the slightest inclination to stammer and stutter.

However, it was her grandfather's clenched jaw that caused the most perplexing worry. He and Maureen Hawkins had made no secret of their attraction to one another. Would he want to stay in the Highlands with her?

Personally, she'd love to have him close since her parents had more or less abandoned her. But Gregor would never allow it.

Fearing she might toss and turn all night, she was relieved to hear Tavish's footsteps on the stairs and the click of the bedroom door as he tried not to make any noise.

She feigned sleep while he undressed, but curled into his warm body once he got into bed.

"I thought ye were asleep," he whispered, drawing her into his arms.

She stretched her leg across his thighs and reached for his manhood. "I canna sleep without my braw Highlander."

"*Nighean dàna*," he growled as his maleness blossomed in her hand.

It wasn't the first time he'd called her a *minx* and she couldn't hear it often enough.

MATCHMAKING

The following week saw a flurry of activity in the glen. The license promised by Dalwhinnie was hand delivered by the Viscount himself. He was given a tour of the distillery and an advance on the two shillings tax as a sign of goodwill.

Gregor privately thought it an unnecessary gesture, but it was Withenshawe's idea, so he kept his opinion to himself. In any case, he spent most of his days supervising the workers Tavish supplied to help open up the Lockie house.

Maureen threw herself wholeheartedly into the task. It was a joy to see her enthusiasm and he couldn't help but think how different his life would have been had he not judged her so harshly. He'd destroyed the ties that bind siblings, no matter how far apart they live.

The bigger problem was he was doing it again. He barely acknowledged Jock's stalwart efforts to assist with the renovations. It was excruciatingly evident the man walked on eggshells when he was with Gregor.

Maureen transformed from a capable whirlwind to a stammering ninny when she, Jock and Gregor were in the same room. They feared his censure.

Jock had voiced his intention to return to the Lowlands within the week. If that happened, Maureen would never be completely happy. Or, and Gregor didn't want to consider the possibility, she might go with him.

One day, when Maureen had gone to discuss curtains with Piper, he made up his mind and cornered Jock in the kitchen. "Would ye nay consider biding here a wee while longer?"

Jock turned his attention away from poking out old ashes in the hearth's firebox. "In Glengeárr, ye mean?"

"Aye. Here. This house is big enough..."

Jock gripped the poker. "What are ye sayin'?"

"Weel," Gregor replied, eyeing the poker. "Ye and Maureen..."

Jock clenched his jaw. "If ye'er implying I'd consider livin' here with ye and yer sister, ye'd best understand I'd want to marry her first."

Marriage hadn't entered into Gregor's plans. But why not? He'd never had a brother. "Have ye asked her?"

"Nay, but I will now," he replied with a grin.

Worried he might have made a big mistake, Gregor attempted a smile.

Then Jock gave him a bear hug and slapped him on the back. "I ken this is hard for ye, but I thank ye."

Gregor's throat constricted. Having a brother-in-law might indeed turn out to be a good thing. He'd banished Freddie Hawkins from his life, but Fate had given him another chance to make his sister happy.

Not so long ago, Kenneth had been present when his cousin and Piper were hand-fasted. Although he'd planned to court Piper, he'd known as she pledged herself to Tavish that all was as it should be.

He felt the same now in Withenshawe's splendid pavilion as he listened to Gregor. His uncle repeated the ancient words of the hand-fasting ceremony he'd performed in London, this time to bind Kenneth's mother to Jock Graham.

Certainly, he'd have preferred she return to London with him, but that was purely for selfish reasons. She could navigate the sometimes treacherous waters of London society with consummate ease. But she belonged in the Highlands, with Jock.

His turmoil had nothing to do with the ceremony, but with his own insistent craving to stay in Scotland and woo Cat.

But neither option was possible. The Ramsay dukedom needed his guidance, and English dukes didn't marry Scottish commoners no matter how often they dreamt of a houseful of raven-haired sons and daughters.

No, he'd return to his life and responsibilities in London, but on one thing he was resolved. He'd make sure any children he sired in the future were proud of their Scottish roots.

Piper squeezed her husband's hand throughout the hand-fasting ceremony. She had to admit she'd been distracted in London when Gregor had recited the words binding her to Tavish. Now, she understood and appreciated their profound meaning in full measure.

And it was her beloved grandfather taking a wife! He'd been widowed so long ago, Piper had no memory of her grandmother. He deserved a fine woman like Maureen Hawkins. What's more, they planned to live just a stone's throw away.

Tavish raised her hand to his lips and whispered, "Ye ken what this means, wife."

Puzzled by his words but not by the glint in his eyes, she replied, "We'll have the house to ourselves until Payton and Niven come home."

"Exactly. Ye can scream as loudly as ye like when we make love."

Her giggle drew a glare from Gregor. "Sorry," she mouthed, elbowing her husband in the ribs.

―∼―

"I wonder where Piper's got to?" Jock said.

"Tavish took her on the long promised private tour of the distillery just before the dancing started," Maureen replied.

"I dinna suppose there's many couples have their wedding breakfast catered by a duke in his luxury pavilion," Jock quipped after a long silence.

Maureen noted the wistful note in his voice. She

reached for his hand under the table. "You're as nervous as I am."

"Aye. Ridiculous for a man my age."

"I'm nervous too. It's because we've both been married before."

"I ken ye had a good marriage wi' Freddie. I suppose..."

She pressed a fingertip to his lips. "This is different, Jock. More comfortable, in a way, and less daunting."

He squeezed her hand. Their gazes met. "We havena discussed it since the voyage," he said. "But I hope ye understand I intend to make ye my wife in every way."

A wave of heat swept over her. She meshed her fingers with his. "I'm counting on it."

∽

Tavish took his time to lead Piper through the distillery. "I want ye to feel the things I feel," he said. " Smell the aromas I inhale every day, feel the chill in the cellar, run yer hands over the rough wood of the barrels."

It took longer than the investors' tour. At every stage in the process, he stopped to kiss and fondle his wife.

She seemed in no hurry to get back to the wedding breakfast, so he made the kisses last.

While he enjoyed the intimate contact, he got the most pleasure out of her genuine interest and her admiration for his part in developing the process. She asked intelligent questions, completely enthralled when they reached the copper kettles. "Beautiful," she breathed, running a hand over the shiny metal. "You put so much effort into your whisky, no wonder it's so fine."

Others had extolled the quality of his whisky, but this woman's words of praise meant more to him than previous accolades.

Homecoming

Kenneth had a cabin to himself on the return voyage. It was cramped but he was glad to be alone. He simply wasn't in the mood for chitchat and even declined Withenshawe's offer of the valet's services. As the days went by, he rarely got out of the bunk. He dreamed every night of the kiss Cat had pecked on his cheek the day he left, and woke with the predictable results on the bed linens.

"I'll ne'er forget ye, Yer Grace," she'd whispered the day they parted.

"Nor I you," he'd admitted, astonished by the longing in her green eyes. "And my name is Kenneth."

Looking back, he realized it wasn't surprising he'd lost Piper. What a pompous ass he'd been, magnanimously granting her leave to address him as Ramsay.

He'd known since the age of three that he was heir to a dukedom. He'd been groomed for it. Though he grieved when his father died, he felt that, at last, he was about to fulfill his destiny. It turned out he was good at being a duke. He enjoyed the role.

Now, he couldn't summon a modicum of enthusiasm for the task.

He wasn't sure how Daisy would take the news of their mother's marriage and her decision to stay in Scotland.

True to his efficient nature, Withenshawe had arranged for a carriage at the London docks, and Kenneth was whisked away to Ramsay House. His fellow duke undertook to seek an audience with the Regent as soon as possible.

Harrison had the front door open as soon as Kenneth stepped down from the carriage. "Welcome home, Your Grace," he said with genuine warmth. "I'll inform Miss Daisy of your arrival."

"No need," Daisy called as she emerged from the drawing room. "Good to see you back safely," she said, giving him a perfunctory hug. He should have expected a cool reception. Daisy had never been an affectionate person. The butler seemed more pleased to see him.

"Where's Mama?" Daisy asked.

He'd hoped for a little time to compose his explanation, but... "She decided to stay in Scotland for a while."

His pouting sister stepped back. "Why on earth would she do that? Did Uncle Gregor badger her?"

"No. Actually, she married Jock Graham and the two of them..."

Daisy swooned at his feet.

∽

Daisy startled awake to find herself in her own room, Mrs. Harrison looming over her with a bottle of smelling salts, her brother hovering anxiously in the shadows.

So, it hadn't been a dream.

She sat up and glared at Kenneth. "How could you allow this to happen?"

He sat on the edge of the bed. "Allow? Do you not think our mother has a mind of her own? She's in love and I'm happy for her."

Daisy's throat constricted. "But how can a person know if they are in love?"

The color drained from her brother's face as he averted his gaze. She'd never seen him look so…bereft.

Then, he looked into her eyes. "Oh, believe me, Daisy, you'll know when you're in love."

Something in him had changed. "You met someone?"

"Aye, but 'twasn't meant to be."

"Because she's a Scot?"

He stood abruptly. "Heavens, no. I would marry the right woman whether she was Scottish or…or…"

She'd touched a raw nerve. They had never confided in each other, so this was new territory. Did she dare tell him? "I thought I was in love, with a Scot."

"Payton King," he replied.

"Was it so obvious? Now, all anyone talks about is Payton and Jasmine. Apparently, they are as thick as thieves."

"The King brothers are still lodging here, I assume," he said, apparently uncomfortable sharing personal feelings. "I need to tell them the good news about the distillery."

Daisy no longer cared about the Kings and their distillery. "I see Niven occasionally, but Payton is too busy with his lady love."

~

Two days later, flanked by Payton and Niven, and feeling more confident than he had on the occasion of his first meeting with the Regent, Kenneth walked into the audience with His Majesty. It seemed unlikely, but he'd swear Prinny had gained even more weight in the interim.

However, judging by the smile on the pudgy royal face, Withenshawe had already informed His Highness of events in Scotland.

He bowed. "May I reintroduce Payton and Niven King, younger brothers of Tavish."

The pair bent the knee.

"Welcome," the Regent declared. "We plan to visit your country in the future. The royal tailors are already fashioning our Highland garb."

Kenneth willed away the vision of the corpulent prince swathed in a kilt.

"So, Ramsay. We've decided to grant the Royal Warrant. With brandy so hard to come by, thanks to Napoleon, it's right and fitting we support the efforts of our own loyal subjects."

The King brothers bristled. They obviously didn't consider themselves loyal subjects of the Hanoverian throne, but it wouldn't be a good idea to get into a discussion about Jacobites.

"Indeed, Your Highness," Kenneth interjected,

heading off whatever Payton had opened his mouth to say.

Prinny surprised Kenneth with his next question. "What's happening with the barrels you plan to bring back from Spain?"

"In our absence, the brothers and my shipping managers have been in communication with the Spaniards," Withenshawe explained. "It seems Napoleon's siege of Cadiz is making things difficult. It's the closest port to the sherry making region."

This was news to Kenneth, although he might have considered the French incursions into Spain would complicate matters and he wasn't overly familiar with Spanish geography.

"We may have to send someone to retrieve the barrels," Withenshawe said. "I've offered one of my ships and Payton has volunteered to go, if it becomes necessary."

Kenneth blinked. Tavish's brother had said nothing of this to him. He dreaded telling Daisy that Payton might sail to war-torn Spain.

"On another matter," the Regent intoned. "We are opposed to the notion of changing the name of our whisky. There can only be one Sovereign and, therefore we prefer the Gaelic *Uachdaran* not be changed."

Pompous ass, was on the tip of Kenneth's tongue but he smiled and bowed his way out of the audience.

"Pompous ass," Payton growled when they were safely away. "But Tavish will be glad the name is to stay the same. The bottles won't have to be changed."

"So am I," Kenneth replied, though his reasoning differed. "'Tis a fitting Highland name."

NEW BEGINNINGS

It wasn't unusual for Niven to feel like the odd-man-out. Payton hadn't invited his input into discussions with Withenshawe's people about the barrels. His offer to go to Spain had come out of the blue without any consultation with his younger brother. At least Tavish made the effort to ask Niven's opinion even if he subsequently overruled it.

If Payton sailed to Spain, Niven might as well return to Scotland. However, from what Cousin Kenneth had told them, it sounded like things were going well enough there without him, and he didn't relish the prospect of sharing a house with Tavish and his wife.

There were still important details of *Uachdaran's* expansion to be taken care of in London. Shipping could be supervised by the duke's capable managers, but there was also the matter of storage and sales. It was all very well bringing the whisky to London but stockpiling it in a warehouse would serve no purpose.

Tackling these challenges was a daunting proposition for the youngest sibling of the family who'd never been trusted with any major decision. But he was confident Kenneth and his man Mainwaring would help him.

Kenneth's visit to Scotland had changed him. He didn't seem the least bit upset about his mother marrying again and staying in Scotland. He'd clearly been very impressed with the distillery and spoke fondly of the people he'd met. Niven didn't know what a Bedouin prince was, but Kenneth had apparently felt like one sleeping in a pavilion that sounded like a big tent.

Kenneth mentioned Catriona a lot. Maybe that was simply because Piper had found a friend in Cat. Payton was so preoccupied with Jasmine, it wasn't surprising he showed no interest in what Cat was up to.

Perhaps the Regent's talk of kilts had prompted Kenneth to order his own Scottish regalia. The pompous prince was obviously enamored with the notion of going to Scotland. Could Kenneth harbor notions of accompanying him? It went without saying a Hanoverian would be well advised to avoid the Highlands.

Niven had heard it said that people who visited Scotland often came home with a trace of a brogue. That was certainly true of Kenneth.

His initial impression of his English cousin was of a stuck up aristocrat. Now, he could envision they might actually become friends, or colleagues at least.

∽

Piper stepped back to admire the new curtains she and Cat—well, mostly Cat—had fashioned for the bedroom window. "Fantastic, and now every window in the house has new curtains."

"Aye," Cat replied. "And it's only taken us three months to accomplish the task."

"True," Piper agreed good-naturedly. "But it was worth waiting for the arrival of the material. I wasn't certain my mother would send what I asked for, but my father's letter said she is getting better every day."

"I'm happy for ye. Yer parents are so far away and to be estranged..."

Piper shook her head. "But my grandfather and Aunty Maureen are close by. Even Uncle Gregor has mellowed."

"Aye, but they're all gettin' on in years. I dinna ken what I'll do when my Grandad passes."

The loneliness in her friend's voice touched Piper's heart. "Has no Highland laddie taken yer fancy? I ken you used to be sweet on Payton..."

She was surprised when tears welled in Cat's eyes. "Do ye miss Payton terribly?"

Cat avoided meeting her sympathetic gaze. "'Tisna Payton I miss."

A thousand possibilities flitted through Piper's brain, but there was only one made sense, though it actually made no sense at all. "Kenneth?"

"Aye," Cat sobbed. "How stupid am I to fall in love wi' a duke, an *Englishmon* to boot?"

"But Kenneth's mother is Scottish," Piper replied, though she recognized she was clutching at straws. Her heart broke for the hopelessness of her friend's feelings.

She was reminded once more of how lucky she was to have found Tavish.

Was the instinctive movement of her hand to rest on her belly that alerted her friend?

"Ye're expectin' a bairn," Cat exclaimed, sniffling back tears.

"Aye," Piper confessed. "But I haven't told Tavish yet. He's been so busy ramping up production at the distillery and fretting about the delay in getting the barrels from Spain."

"When do ye plan to tell him?"

"Tonight."

∼

After a long and frustrating day in the distillery, Tavish was so exhausted he could barely stay awake to eat the supper Piper had prepared. But his wee wife was proud of her progress with the wood stove, so he persevered. She'd been a bit touchy of late, perhaps annoyed he was spending most of his days in the distillery. "The mutton's delicious," he tried.

"I thought it was chewy," she replied, pushing aside her plate.

"Ye've hardly eaten any of it," he said.

"I'm not that hungry," she replied. "I think I'll just go to bed."

Left alone, he wondered what was amiss. Lately, they hadn't made love as often. He'd been content to hold her in his arms every night, too tired to do much else.

Aye, that was it. She was a passionate woman who needed more loving.

He was bone weary but his manhood agreed it was a good idea. He finished his meal, blew out the candles and tackled the stairs.

To his surprise, Piper was sitting up in bed, the linens pulled up to cover her nakedness. The gilt frames of the oil paintings she'd hung on the walls glowed in the light of the lone candle. "Ye've made this room a lot cozier," he said as he stripped off his clothes and folded them neatly —a small effort on his part he'd learned she appreciated.

He climbed into bed and drew her into his arms, but she was stiff and too quiet. Something was bothering her, but he was mystified. Then he saw the new curtains. Of course! Women tended to pout when a man didn't notice their efforts around the house. "I love the new curtains," he enthused.

To his dismay, she burst into tears. Evidently, he taken too long to notice the window coverings. "What is it, my love?" he asked.

"I'm pregnant," she wailed.

In that moment, Tavish was the king of the world, and the biggest fool in Christendom. "Are ye nay happy to be carryin' my bairn?" he asked reluctantly.

"I'm thrilled about it," she replied hoarsely. "I don't know why I am crying."

He lay down and gathered her into his arms. "Ye've made me a happy man," he whispered. "I canna wait to meet my son."

She cuddled into him. "What if it's a girl?"

"Weel, Glengeárr could do wi' few more bonnie lasses."

"Speaking of bonnie lasses, I found out today that Cat and Kenneth..."

"Aye. I noticed and so did Aunty Maureen. She's already plotting how to bring them together."

FOOTNOTES

I learned a lot about distilling whisky in the course of writing this story. I took many of the steps in the process from the practices of modern-day single malt distillers in Scotland, and I'm indebted to them for providing so much detail on their websites.

I'd also like to thank the members of my critique group for their invaluable insights—Reggi Allder, Jacquie Biggar, LizAnn Carson and Sylvie Grayson, all accomplished authors.

Thanks also go to my beta reader extraordinaire, Maria McIntyre, and my PA Alison Pridie.

And a special thank you to a reader, Ingrid, who pitched me the idea for this series.

~

THE REGENT DID EVENTUALLY FULFILL his wish to travel to Scotland, but not until 1822 when he was King George IV. It was the first visit of a reigning monarch to Scotland in nearly two centuries, the last being by Charles II for his Scottish coronation in 1651. The visit increased the king's popularity in Scotland. However, it was Sir Walter Scott's organization of the visit, with the inclusion of tartan pageantry, that was to have a lasting influence. The tartan kilt was elevated to become part of Scotland's national identity.

Napoleon

The Little Emperor's march through Europe is a complicated tale of innumerable battles fought over a period of almost ten years. Some took place on the Iberian Peninsula. The French siege of Cadiz (1810-1812) is of particular interest to us and our story. Jerez, the sherry capital of the world is located not far from Cadiz. The French eventually abandoned the siege and Cadiz holds the distinction of being the only city that ever withstood a siege by Napoleon's troops.

Various coalitions were formed to defeat Napoleon and he finally met his fate at Waterloo in 1815.

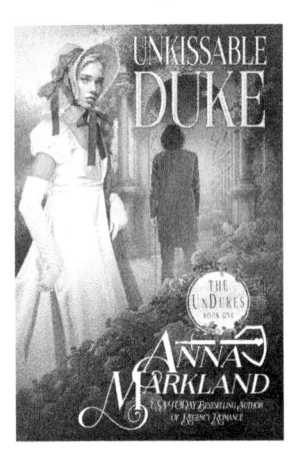

Some of my books deal more directly with the Battle of Waterloo. The hero of Unkissable Duke, Alex Harcourt, returns to England severely injured and badly disfigured. As far as he is concerned, his life is over. It takes the love of a good woman to prove him wrong.

EVERY EARL HAS a Silver Lining features a career soldier charged with guarding Napoleon on the remote island of St. Helena. He is obliged to return to England when he unexpectedly inherits an earldom. He doesn't expect the beautiful widow of the previous earl to still be in residence when he arrives.

AS AN AMATEUR GENEALOGIST (aka an addict of family tree research) I became obsessed with tracing my English roots back to the Norman Conquest in the 11th century.

This turned out to be a pipe dream since I am not descended from the nobility and records were not kept for "common folks" until much later. Even then, early parish records are often indecipherable.

As a result, I began to write stories about a noble medieval family I conjured from my imagination. The Montbryces were born.

Like many people, I had an inner compulsion to write one good book. What was originally intended as that one book about my fictional family eventually became the 12-book series, The Montbryce Legacy.

In other words, writing superseded genealogy as my

principal addiction, and I have since published more than 60 novels and novellas. Almost all are historical romances that feature Vikings, Highlanders, medieval knights, Elizabethan goldsmiths or Regency aristocrats. You can find more details on my website https://annamarkland.com/.

I've lived most of my life in Canada, though I was born in the UK. An English grammar school education instilled in me a love of European history which continues to this day. While I may boast of being a proud Canadian, I'm still a Lancashire lass at heart.

Before becoming a full-time writer, I was an elementary school teacher, a job I loved. I then worked as administrator for a world-wide disaster relief organization.

I love cats, although I haven't been able to bring myself to adopt another one since unexpectedly losing Topaz a few years ago.

I have few domestic skills. You'll notice most of my heroines hate sewing!

I try to follow three simple writing guidelines. I give my characters free rein to tell their story, which often turns out to be different from the original version in my head. I'm a firm believer in love at first sight. My protagonists may initially deny the attraction but, eventually, my heroes and heroines find their soul mates. It seems only natural then to include scenes of intimacy enjoyed by people who love each other deeply. I believe such intimacy is wholesome. Historical accuracy is important to me, although I have been known to tweak history when necessary. I write romance because I find happy endings very satisfying.

You can find me on all the usual social media platforms. On Facebook as Anna Markland and Anna Markland Novels, on Pinterest and BookBub as Anna Markland. I also have a reader group on Facebook called Markland's Merrymakers and new members are always welcome.

Printed in Great Britain
by Amazon